Praise for Scrolls of Cridhe Volume 1-Highland Winds

Awesome set of books. All very well written and make you want for more. I really enjoyed the whole set."
-jmiller, Amazon reader review

Great writing by some great authors! The novella format was nice since you didn't have to commit as much reading time to each story. That said, I will be revisiting these stories again and again.
-Deborah Yanofsky, Amazon reader review

I liked each and every one of the stories in this set. These stories made me laugh and cry and they even made me understand some of the bad guys and why they were being that way.
-Bookwoman, Amazon reader review

The Taming of Mairi MacKenzie

A Scrolls of Cridhe Novella

By:
Sue-Ellen Welfonder

Duncurra LLC
www.duncurra.com

Copyright 2014 by Sue-Ellen Welfonder

ISBN-10:1942623046
ISBN-13:978-1-942623-04-5

Produced in the USA

Other Books by Sue-Ellen Welfonder

Written as Allie Mackay

The Ravenscraig Legacy Series

Highlander in Her Bed (Book 1)

Highlander in Her Dreams (Book 2)

Tall, Dark and Kilted (Book 3)

Some Like it Kilted (Book 4)

**Other Novellas by
Sue-Ellen Welfonder**

Falling in Time

The Seventh Sister

Dedication

For my beloved Em –

my brightest shining star.

"There is no magic greater than love, but woe betide any who'd claim I said so."

~ Devorgilla of Doon, cailleach, wise woman, Highland legend

The Banshee of the Glen of Winds

Deep in the most remote bounds of the Western Highlands, keen-eyed wayfarers might notice fissures in the cold, bare rock of the wild, soaring mountains. Dark and forbidding, these crevices only beckon to those of stout heart and steely will, for many tales are spun about what might dwell within such ancient, forgotten places.

Some say the openings lead to the far edge of the world. Others argue that these hills are part of Kintail, territory of the great Clan MacKenzie, reminding folk that the clan's leader, Duncan, the Black Stag of Kintail, would cut down any man who'd dare cast a slur against the land he's known to love and guard so passionately. Only the bravest souls then note that even the legendary MacKenzie chieftain rarely passes this way, and that he warns his people to tread gently if ever they must cross these savage and rock-strewn peaks.

For somewhere in their midst, lies the Glen of Winds, a steep-sided abyss of crags, knolls, and heather, where the ever-racing wind carries the lost souls of the damned, leaving them there to wallow in loneliness and solitude.

No one can say for sure.

And few wish to seek answers.

It's enough to know that the wind does wail and moan here, blowing cold, dark, and endlessly.

Mist often swirls and eddies in the tiny Glen of Winds, and some have sworn earlier times can be glimpsed if one peers hard enough into the half-light. The truth is a centuries-old broch stands hidden in the glen. Known by the MacKenzies as Dunwynde, it's rumored to be the dwelling place of a fearsome, wild-eyed banshee.

Indeed, her cries have been heard echoing off the cliffs.

Souls unfortunate enough to have seen her, claim she has hair and eyes of fire, and that her face is so bleak that if one looks upon her too long, madness descends. The banshee then celebrates, watching in satisfaction as the doomed wander away, forever lost in the glen's sea of huge, granite boulders and whirling mist.

The banshee's presence keeps visitors from setting foot in the Glen of Winds.

Only a fool would risk encountering her.

Or perhaps a desperate man.

For if one is tireless in the quest to learn the glen's secrets, other fascinating tales are sometimes revealed. Stories of a beautiful, reclusive woman, bold, tempestuous, and just as wild-eyed as the banshee she's reputed to be. She's said to possess a strange and powerful gift, the astonishing ability to bring the dead back to life.

Her name is Mairi MacKenzie.

And she sees her talent as a curse.

Dunwynde is her refuge; the glen her secret, well-guarded home. Many are her reasons for hiding from the world. Clan MacKenzie makes certain she isn't disturbed, protecting her as one of their dearest treasures. Only Mairi knows how unworthy she is of her clan's devotion.

A shame one man is so determined to meet her.

And that he's one of Scotland's greatest warriors, even if circumstance has kept him from lifting a sword in years. Men still remember him and bards sing his praises. Women adore him, but he's shunned them with a vengeance more fierce than his refusal to wield a blade.

All that is really left to him is his love for his clan and his home.

Now he stands to lose them as well.

Unless the Glen of Winds banshee will help him.

Knowing he must save everything he holds dear, he uses his warrior skills to find her. But dangers of the past are lurking and if Mairi gives the warrior what he needs, she will doom herself forevermore.

Prologue

"There's a dark wind blowing through your lands, that I say you." Devorgilla of Doon, Scotland's most revered cailleach, stood importantly before the solar's hearth fire, and peered at her host, the equally far-famed Duncan MacKenzie, Black Stag of Kintail. "Blood will soon flow, a great evil that would smite innocents."

A tiny, black-garbed woman with a wizened face, a whir of white-gray hair, and bright blue eyes, what truly set her apart were the red plaid laces she used to tie her black boots. And, perhaps, how spry she was, considering her formidable age. Years, possibly even centuries, that no wise man would risk mentioning.

Often referred to as simply Herself, Devorgilla commanded respect.

Here, in the heart of the Black Stag's lair, Duncan's own privy solar in his beloved loch-girt stronghold, Eilean Creag, that posed a problem.

Duncan ruled his territory with an iron hand.

Just now, he didn't care for how the orange-red glow from his peat fire edged the cailleach. The lurid, flickering light gave her an otherworldly air that didn't sit at all well with him. It also displeased him that he was certain she knew and had taken advantage.

Hadn't she hobbled right to the hearth upon entering the room?

So Duncan frowned, something he did well.

If she thought to bedevil him with her witchy ways, he'd treat her to his infamous scowls.

In careful measure, of course.

"You have journeyed here in vain, great lady." He used the title he knew she expected, not wishing to grieve her more than was necessary. "My lands are at peace."

"That they are, indeed," came a deep Sassunach voice from across the room. "Nor have there been any troublesome stirrings at my own Balkenzie Castle. I keep southern Kintail secured for you."

"As well you should." His mood worsening, Duncan looked sharply at the tall, scar-faced knight who'd claimed the solar's best chair.

It was Duncan's own, crafted of heavy black oak and richly carved. Sir Marmaduke Strongbow, Duncan's longtime friend and brother-in-law by marriage, sprawled there now, his long legs stretched before him, his usual air of imperturbability so annoying that Duncan's head began to ache. How typical that the lout would choose the same afternoon as Devorgilla to darken his door.

Duncan almost believed his friend also possessed crafty powers.

He just hoped Sir Marmaduke wouldn't mention his patrols along a certain glen.

"I've seen no cause for concern up near the Glen of Winds either," the fiend said, doing just that. "Even so, we should heed Devorgilla's warning."

Duncan glared at him.

Sir Marmaduke lifted his wine cup, sipped with irritating deliberation.

"He is a wise man, your friend." The crone preened, sounding smug.

"No man would dare set foot in the Glen of Winds." Duncan was certain. He made sure his mien and stance said so. Having positioned himself at one of the solar's window embrasures, he kept his legs braced apart, his arms folded, as he met the crone's piercing blue gaze.

He also took care not to glance at his lady wife, Linnet. She'd been silent until now, setting the room's only table with platters of oatcakes and cheese, a few ewers of fine Rhenish wine. He knew without looking that Linnet believed the crone.

He did, too, though he wasn't of a mind to say so.

He'd learned long ago that wherever Devorgilla appeared, trouble soon followed. Sometimes he suspected she conjured the mayhem, taking pleasure in spreading mischief. He wouldn't put anything past her.

He also appreciated the peace that had settled over Kintail in recent years.

Quiet days he meant to maintain.

For sure, a dark wind was coming. But it wasn't a war-band or a horde of unholy ghoulies. He made certain that every man, woman, and child, in his territory slept safely. The blackness descending was his temper and only his grudging respect for the cailleach kept it at bay.

"'Twas the Glen of Winds I saw in my cauldron's steam." The crone swelled her chest, her thin shoulders squaring. "It rose before me clear as day, a narrow, steep-sided defile with jumbles of broken rock, thick heather, gorse, and bog myrtle. It was a wild and inaccessible place, unmistakable. The dark winds came from everywhere, black mists whirling about me, my ears aching from the screams and howls-"

"To be sure, you heard wailing." He had her now. "A banshee dwells there, as all men know. Nothing stirs in that benighted place except her cries and the souls of the doomed." He didn't say his clan spread the rumors. If she was as wise as she loved to boast, she knew.

If his Sassunach friend or his lady wife revealed the glen's secret, there'd be hell to pay.

He flashed a look at them both.

Sir Marmaduke had helped himself to a handful of oatcakes and was calmly enjoying one, not at all looking as if the greatest cailleach in the land had just proclaimed doom and destruction was about to befall their beloved Kintail.

His lovely wife, still so desirable with her thick braid of glossy red-gold hair, and the fine heathery scent that aye wafted about her, was just stepping back into the solar, carrying a jeweled flagon of Duncan's best uisage beatha. Fiery Highland spirits he agreed would be most welcome before Devorgilla took her leave.

What wasn't welcome was catching the look Linnet cast at the crone.

"Did you see aught else?" his wife wanted to know, speaking in a way Duncan didn't like.

He knew the tone well.

It meant she, too, had seen something.

As the seventh daughter of a seventh daughter, she was gifted – or cursed – with the second sight; a talent that still had the power to rattle him to the bones, however long they'd been married.

She poured a small cup of uisge beatha and took it to the cailleach. "Anything at all?"

"There do be more, aye." Devorgilla accepted the libation, slid another pointed look at Duncan as she sipped. "Your men patrol the hills about the glen," she said, proving as always that she knew things she shouldn't. "You'd best have a word with them. They should be aware that a ne'er before wickedness approaches."

"I will strengthen their number." Duncan nodded, agreeing to keep the peace, secretly resenting an old woman telling him what to do.

Any foulness that thought to enter Kintail was aye met with the sharp edge of a sword, the drawn steel of many blades, all of them expertly wielded.

Such was enough.

"The men who watch that area are my best warriors." Duncan unfolded his arms and reached to rub the back of his neck, which was beginning to pain him.

He turned slightly, glancing out the embrasure's arched window. It was a fine afternoon and Loch Duich shone like blue glass in the cold autumn sun. Beyond, for Eilean Creag claimed an island in the loch, the great hills of Kintail stretched on and on, dressed now in shades of burnished red and gold. But a thick mist was gathering on the higher peaks and the swirling blue-gray mass gave him a chill. The Glen of Winds was hidden deep inside those rugged, trackless heights. And on such days, especially so close to gloaming, the wee defile would disappear beneath the fog.

No man would know the glen existed.

And that was why it'd been chosen as the refuge of one of his most precious kinswomen.

Duncan's scowl returned, along with a cold, unpleasant tightness in his gut. Turning away from the window, he hooked his thumbs in his sword belt and addressed the tiny, black-garbed cailleach.

"Sir Marmaduke often rides with the men who guard the Glen of Winds." He glanced at the Sassunach, letting a curt nod acknowledge his friend's renown and experience. "Only a fool would challenge such a patrol. Nor will they allow any man to cross into the glen."

"So I knew!" Devorgilla wagged a finger. "See you, there is one man they must give entry, a great warrior whose fame is almost as great as your own.

"And his," she added, giving Sir Marmaduke a bright, twinkly-eyed smile.

Duncan waited, not swayed by her flattery.

"Who is this paragon?" He didn't know why he asked, for Devorgilla ever answered in riddles.

"He is the man who will repel the dark winds," she returned, proving him right.

Duncan glared back at her, his anger rising. "There is a treasure in that glen." He wasn't about to say more. "If I dinnae ken who to trust, no stranger will enter the Glen of Winds."

"He won't be a stranger when your men see him." The crone persisted in speaking riddles.

"If he's not known to me, he's an outsider." Duncan wouldn't risk his kin. "My men will have orders to run him through with a spear."

"I believe I know who he is." Linnet appeared at his side, slid her arm gently through his. "I have seen him," she admitted, leaning into him softly as she always did, calming him as no one else could. "It happened in my herbarium, only moments before Devorgilla arrived.

"There wasn't time to tell you." She looked up at him, the truth in her eyes. A rich brown, but flecked with gold, they were still the most beautiful eyes he'd ever seen. They were also expressive, and never ever lied. She used them now to hold his gaze. "I have never before seen this man and I cannot say his name, but a fine silvery light edged him, letting me know he is good."

"That be him!" Devorgilla beamed. "Had silver shining all round him, he did."

"Saints, Maria, and Joseph!" Duncan stepped away from his wife, roared his favorite curse. Scowling at Devorgilla, he shoved his hands through his hair. "You would have me tell me my guards to look for a man who is good and walks about wreathed in silver?"

Sure his men would hold him for addled, he pinched the bridge of his nose and closed his eyes. He drew a long breath, hoped that when he looked again, he'd find himself in his bed, this entire misbegotten day naught but an unpleasant dream.

"Perhaps the man is a knight?" Sir Marmaduke's voice rose from across the solar, shattering the possibility. "Knights wear mail, could appear to shine like silver."

"Is that so?" Duncan glowered at him.

Devorgilla smiled at the Sassunach, bobbed her grizzled head. "He surely is a knight, and a much honored one," she trilled, her eyes lighting. "But the silver ringing him is his goodness, no' a coat of mail."

"Then he'd best don one because my men will fall upon him when he appears." Duncan strode over to the table and snatched up the usage beatha flagon, pouring himself a large measure and tossing it down in one long swig.

Dragging the back of his hand across his mouth, he turned back to the others. "Your champion is a dead man, Devorgilla. Lest you-"

"Aye, that he may be." She threw a glance at Linnet, then looked again at Duncan. "Whether he's dead or no', isn't how your men will recognize him."

Duncan spoke through gritted teeth. "Then how will they?"

Devorgilla jutted her chin. "He carries a broken sword."

"Then he can be no great warrior." That Duncan knew.

"Ah, but he once was," Devorgilla informed him, again wagging her finger. "The rent blade is his penance. He seeks the Glen of Winds to cast off his shame." She lowered her hand, glancing round at them all. "Regrettably, he isn't the only soul heading there.

"But he is the one who shall save your treasure," she finished, looking pleased.

"I see." Duncan did, leastways he hoped so.

He might have a temper, but he wasn't a fool.

He understood something of broken warriors. Great men who'd made poor choices and sought redemption. Once, many long moons ago, he'd belonged to their number. If Devorgilla and his lady wife were sure this faceless fighter was worthy, he wouldn't harass him.

As for the rest…

He'd take measures to safeguard kith and kin, as always.

Satisfied, he smoothed his proud MacKenzie plaid and gave the cailleach his word. "My men will be instructed to allow this warrior passage across our lands, even into the Glen of Winds."

He glanced at Sir Marmaduke, satisfied when his friend inclined his head.

"It is agreed, the man with a broken sword is welcome in Kintail." Duncan waited for any final arguments.

When none came, he nodded. "So be it."

Chapter 1

Mairi MacKenzie knew the moment a stranger entered the glen. She felt a shifting in the air, a ripple down her spine. So she stilled before the broch's central fire, and quietly set aside the long wooden ladle she'd just lifted off her table. Tending her cook-pot could wait, her dinner mattered less than her safety. She might not possess the gift so many believed she had, an ability to bring the dead back to life, but she was fond of living.

Necessity had taught her caution, honing her senses.

She'd heard the telltale crunch of a horse's hooves on pebbled stone. She'd also caught the creak of saddle leather, the jingle of a harness. Her fine-tuned ears picked up the sounds through chinks in the walls of the half-ruinous broch that served as her home.

A rough shelter, to be sure. Even so, Dunwynde guarded her well, its age-smoothed stones protecting her through the long, endless-seeming moons since she'd left everything she'd known to become the banshee of this fearsome defile.

A mythic terror few would risk troubling.

Now...

Someone had breached her sanctuary, and the knowledge alarmed her greatly.

She shivered, the cold coming from within. Then she stepped away from her cauldron of thick, simmering stew, and crossed the broch's circular main room to the low lintelled entry. A heavy length of hide hung there, as good a door as needed in this benighted place, so shunned by men. Behind her, peat haze hung in the air, the earthy-sweet scent not soothing her as on most days. For the first time she could remember, the chill wind that aye raced through the glen, struck ill-ease into her heart, even prickling her skin.

There could be no reason for anyone to visit Dunwynde.

For someone to seek her was even more unsettling.

She didn't want to seek a new hideaway.

She'd been so grateful to have found succor here, regaining the calm and quietude that had been stolen from her when she'd been chased from her cottage at Drumbell village. Branded the devil's own mistress, she'd fled to her clan chieftain, Duncan MacKenzie, the Black Stag of Kintail. A good and strong leader, he'd settled her at Dunwynde, vowing that no harm would come to her within its ancient embrace. She even felt a bond to the broch's earliest dwellers, sensing they'd welcomed her to the strange, tower-like structure they'd built so long ago. She also liked the glen's wildness, its rugged splendor a balm to her soul.

She didn't care if folk thought her a banshee.

Not if such a guise kept her peace.

Hoping it wasn't about to be broken, she gripped the edge of the door-flap, easing the leather aside. The glen stretched long and narrow before her, its sides tall and sheer, the ground rock-strewn and hemmed with birches. Mist rolled everywhere, making it difficult to see the track that twisted down from the windswept pass so high above her. If anyone rode there, spray from several plunging cataracts and the mist hid the intruder from view.

Even so, she reached for the short sword propped by the door. She raised it defensively, her heart thumping hard in her chest at the rustling of autumn-brittle leaves, the snap of a twig.

She saw no one.

Yet she knew someone approached.

Mairi bit her lip, wary. She hadn't imagined the noise. As if the gods wished to send another warning, the crunch of footsteps on stone came again. Not a horse's step this time, but the unmistakable tread of a man. He was closer now, coming through the mist-drenched glen, and making for Dunwynde.

Tightening her grip on the sword, Mairi prepared to swing if she must.

She hoped she needn't.

Her heart thundered, disbelief warring with her dread.

The Black Stag, as her chieftain was known, sent frequent patrols along the perimeters of her tiny, rockbound refuge. His men were hand-picked, fierce, and battle-hardened. One of them, her chieftain's captain of the guard, Sir Marmaduke Strongbow, had once been hailed as one of the realm's greatest swordsmen. He was still revered, his fame undimmed. Such champions would never allow anyone to disturb her. Whoever approached, must've gained entry by stealth. Like as not, a poor misguided soul hoping she could cast miracles.

Or her enemy had found her, a threat she couldn't ignore.

Hatred and envy were powerful emotions and she'd roused both in a truly formidable foe.

Sorcha Bell's face flashed across her mind, the healer's angry, twisted mien letting Mairi's courage swell, her own fury steeling her backbone. Her heart still pounded, and her mouth had gone dry, but she stood taller. Unafraid, she hooked back the door's leather curtain and stepped outside, into the half-light.

She saw the sword before she saw the man.

Shining brightly in the gloom, the weapon's blade revealed that no one need fear its swing.

The sword was broken, more than half of its proud length missing.

Before she could wonder why, the mist parted and the man wearing the rent sword strode into view. He was tall, powerfully built, and clearly a warrior, though his proud features were merely grim-set, not aggressive. Mist whirled around him and Mairi would've sworn each tendril sparkled, but it was only the sheen of his mail shirt, and perhaps the glint of the silver Thor's hammer hanging at his neck. His arm rings also shone brightly, the number of them indicating his status as a fighting man of great skill.

The plaid slung boldly over his shoulder told her he was a Highlander, while his dark good looks would've trapped her breath in her chest if she still allowed herself to acknowledge the passion that once ran so hotly in her blood. Even so, she couldn't deny the jolt of awareness that hit her when his gaze locked on hers.

Once, long ago, she'd have embraced such a powerful attraction, the natural urge to touch, taste, and melt into his warrior body, the intimacy exciting not just her flesh but searing her soul.

Mairi took a deep breath, steadying herself against the wild beating of her heart, the racing of her blood. The warrior was almost upon her, his strides purposeful. Whoever he was, his eyes were deeply shadowed, their grimness leaving no doubt that he came as a miracle seeker.

Like so many before him.

All that set him apart from the others was the huge dog at his side. A massive brute, the beast could've been a wolf-or-deerhound, though a strain of something more savage gave him the look of a war-dog capable of tearing out a man's throat at a single command.

Mairi felt only a surge of love for him.

He could have been her own beloved Clyde, her much-missed companion who had indeed once been a war-dog, until she'd found and nursed him back to health. Clyde's years with her had been far too short, but he'd taught her that the softest heart could beat beneath the fiercest exterior, so she didn't fear the stranger's dog.

She *was* wary of the warrior.

So she straightened her shoulders and started forward, not wanting him to reach her door. She didn't brandish her sword at him. Like as not, he'd flick it aside as easily if brushing lint from his sleeve. But it didn't hurt for him to see that she was prepared to defend herself.

She just chose to do so with a casual tone and an unconcerned mien.

"Are you lost, sir?" She knew he wasn't. "Not many wayfarers come this way."

"I am no' a traveler, my lady, nor have I erred direction." He stopped before her, fixing her with his intense, dark eyes. "I am Sir Gare MacTaggert of Blackrock Castle on the other side of this fair realm, and I came to your Glen of Winds to seek the aid of its banshee."

That I knew, good sir, and you can leave now.

The glen's banshee cannot help you.

"There is no such being here." Mairi gave him a third version of the truth. "You have journeyed for naught. I dwell in this glen with my husband," she allowed herself the lie. "He will return anon-"

"Lady Mairi." A slight smile lifted the corners of his mouth. "I was told you'd attempt to send me away, and I ken you aren't married." He glanced down at his dog, then back at her, his smile now gone. "Troll and I come in peace and mean you no harm. Your chieftain's captain of the guard, Sir Marmaduke, and his men, granted us passage across their lands and into this glen.

"I spoke with them only a short while ago." He glanced up at the cliff-tops, now thick with lowering mist and clouds. "They were good enough to take my horse back to your chief's Eilean Creag Castle for stabling and care while I am in the Glen of Winds."

"You cannot think to stay here." Mairi tried to look away from him, but couldn't. His gaze was too compelling. "I dwell alone, my broch too small for a guest." She waited as the dog rubbed against her, bumping his great head at her hand. "Besides, you've truly come in vain. There isn't a banshee to aid you or anyone.

"The banshee is me." Mairi stood straighter, ignoring his dog. "She is a tall tale spun to keep intruders from disturbing my peace. No more, no less, see you?"

"So I was told, my lady." He inclined his head in acknowledgment, another slight smile curving his lips. A sad one this time. "In truth, it was you who drew me here, no' a myth. Your reputation as a healer is great, reaching even to my lands in Scotland's distant northeastern bounds. I believe you can help me, leastways I have prayed to the gods that is so. If you will but give me your ear, I swear to depart at first light should you decide against aiding me."

Mairi frowned, her heart beating wildly again.

The dog, Troll, was leaning into her, staring up at her with friendly, hopeful eyes. His master, Sir Gare, towered over her, a terribly appealing flicker of hope in his own gaze chipping away at her resistance.

Mairi folded her arms, every protective instinct she had screaming caution.

She didn't want to find any man appealing.

For sure, not one who would turn on her as soon as it became clear that she couldn't restore life to his loved one.

"I must ask you to leave." There, she'd said what she must.

Go before my heart yearns for you as fiercely as my woman's body already does.

Dear heavens, he smelled of sandalwood, clean wool, leather, cold air and man, and the heady blend was fuzzing her wits, making her vulnerable. Worse, he had a way of looking at her that made her feel as if he'd actually touched her, and in intimate, sensual ways!

Mairi's pulse quickened, a tingling, long-forgotten warmth pooling low by her thighs.

No virgin, she'd once loved well and had never denied herself passion. She recognized the danger of this man, with his alluring scent and potent virility. His tall, well-muscled body, surely hard as iron. His strong, beautiful hands that reminded her of the pleasures a skilled lover's questing fingers could give a woman.

Joys she hadn't known in so long.

"See here, I can do nothing for you," she started again, sure she was glowering. "Nor can you sleep here." She indicated the rock-sided glen, the boulder-strewn ground. "Even if I wished you to stay, there isn't enough bracken to make the thinnest pallet."

His gaze locked with hers, and something in his expression told her she was losing. "Troll and I can sleep on the ground." He spoke as if everything was settled. "We have done so most nights of our journey. I need no more than my plaid, and Troll is well-furred enough to no' feel the rocks beneath him."

"Very well." Mairi nodded, sure resistance was futile. "But you'll leave on the morrow."

"If you say you cannae help me, aye."

"I'm telling you that now."

"It is said you have brought back the breath of life to the coldest of the damned." His words pierced her heart, making her soul ache. "Your fame is on every bard's tongue, the wonders you have wrought, the miracles-"

"The tales are untrue." Mairi tucked her hair behind an ear, kept her chin raised. "No one can bring the dead back to life."

"Yet you have done so."

"Aye, but-"

He stepped closer and gripped her arm, his touch sending ripples of awareness through her. "I wouldn't be here if my request wasn't dire, my lady. All I ask is that you restore-"

"I regret you've lost someone." She did, especially that she couldn't do what he wanted.

She knew the pain of heartache.

So before she could think better of it, she lifted her hand to his face and touched his cheek, slid her fingers along his beard. "I do wish I could help you, but all I can offer is my sympathy."

"You misunderstand." He caught her hand, lacing their fingers, squeezing tight. Determination burned in his eyes. "The dead I want you to revive is a man who hasn't truly died. He stands before you."

"You?" Mairi blinked. "Now I am quite confused."

"You willnae be." He glanced aside, drew a deep breath. "My lady, I have lost all feeling inside me. I would that you use your skill to rekindle my will to live."

Mairi didn't know what to say.

"I would be whole again." He turned back to her, the look on his face making it impossible to refuse him. "Dinnae deny me."

"I won't." Mairi couldn't believe her consent. "I'll do what I can," she added, making it worse.

She didn't know where to begin to help him.

She just knew she must.

~ * ~

About the same time, but high on the windswept peaks above the glen, a tiny black-garbed woman stood as close to the cliff edge as she dared, and peered down at the ill-starred pair beneath her.

She was Devorgilla of Doon, the Highlands' most far-famed cailleach and wise woman, and she'd plied her formidable skills since before time was. She worked tirelessly for the greater good, and rarely had two souls needed her more than her latest charges: The tall warrior with his broken sword and the lass who shouldn't sleep alone, only the wind to say her goodnight.

Such loneliness was unnatural.

And the man should have a warm and loving woman at his side, not cold, sundered steel.

Tsk'ing, Devorgilla hitched her skirts and inched a bit closer to the drop-off. She swatted at the whirling mist, mumbled a few words to dispel enough for her to see more clearly. Satisfied, she set her hands on her hips and leaned forward, studying the couple.

Theirs was a hard path, she knew.

Gare MacTaggert, for he'd lost so much. Mairi MacKenzie because she'd never had a lot to begin with. Such misfortune had drawn her to them for she was a born matchmaker, though some called her a meddler.

Either way, she did as she pleased.

Few could deny she was aye right in the end.

Hoping to keep it that way, she slid a glance at her companion and helpmate, Somerled, a little red fox standing close beside her.

"I do believe the lass saw our warding sparkles," she mused, certain of it. She'd seen Mairi narrow her gaze on the silvery glitter in the air about the warrior; the sparkles all that remained of the goodwill charm she'd cast over him. A caution, no more; a quiet way to make certain that the Black Stag's men not only allowed him entry into the Glen of Winds, but also received him as a friend.

Someone they could trust, the wards letting them see him as he truly was.

A good and valiant man.

"By all the fates, she saw." Devorgilla nodded sagely. "Do you no' agree, laddie?"

Somerled blinked in response, his gaze earnest.

"She is more gifted than she knows, eh?" Devorgilla reached down to stroke her friend's silky red fur. "Thought it was the gleam of his mail, she did! No bother. The last bits will be gone anon," she added, pushing back her sleeves and cracking her knotty knuckles.

"Now look closely," she urged the fox. "Show me any lingering sparkles."

It pinched her pride to need such aid, but given her years, her eyes weren't what they'd once been.

Understanding, Somerled again fixed his attention on the warrior. He eyed him carefully, and then raised his foot, pawing the air and pointing at each wayward glint of floating silver.

Devorgilla responded in kind, wriggling a gnarled finger at each sparkle. She only had to will it so, for the charm residue to vanish.

She counted twenty glitter-dots. Then they were gone, nary a shiver of magick remaining.

"Our work is done, laddie." Mightily pleased, she stepped away from the cliff edge and gave a little cackle of glee. "They are on their own now. We have only given them a wee nudge. Whether they do aught about it is up to them."

That Devorgilla knew with all the wisdom in her grizzled head.

Somerled apparently agreed, for he was already sending expectant glances at the plaid-covered basket packed with their dinner – a fine roasted gannet, the succulent seabird one of the crone's favorites, green cheese, oatcakes, two cooked eggs, and a flagon of heather ale.

"They be good victuals, eh?" Devorgilla hobbled over to the basket, rewarding her friend with a tasty gannet tidbit. "Lady Linnet aye treats us well."

Somerled angled his head and tapped the basket with his paw, in clear accord.

Before Devorgilla could give him another piece of gannet, the little fox looked aside to peer at the greatest of Kintail's hills, massive, rock-bound heights as mist-cloaked as the cliffs above the Glen of Winds. The intensity of his gaze and his perked ears warned that he saw more than the blowing mist.

"So we're yet needed, are we?" Devorgilla glanced at the rugged peaks, wariness spreading through her ancient bones.

As always, her wee friend was right to be concerned.

Trouble brewed on the horizon, and its darkness was drifting near, making its way to the Glen of Winds, its purpose pure and deadly evil.

"Ach, laddie, you'd best tell me what you ken." She bent to tighten her red plaid bootlaces, flashing a look at the fox as she did so. "I ken fine ye see more than I do," she admitted, somewhat grudgingly.

Somerled blinked and twitched his tail, a nod to his own pride.

When Devorgilla straightened, he did as she'd bid him, fixing her with his deep and piercing gaze. Ever her talebearer, he used their special bond to rely what he'd gleaned on recent roamings. He also shared what he'd learned just now, peering into the distance.

Grateful, Devorgilla pressed a hand against her hip, giving him her fullest attention, listening not with her ears, but her heart.

What she heard worried her.

Yet fate was inexorable, all things happening for a reason. Nudges and the dash of a charm here and there were fine, harming no one and aiding many.

But every man had to walk his own path, choosing well or otherwise.

Bad things happened to those who sought to bend that rule.

And she hadn't reached her impressive number of years by behaving imprudently.

So she dusted her hands, brushed down her skirts, and adjusted her new black woolen cloak, Duncan MacKenzie's parting gift to her; the proud chieftain's thanks for telling him about the man with the broken sword.

"Come, laddie, we have done all we can here." Devorgilla retrieved their food basket, hooking it on her arm. "It is time for us to return to Doon, for thon pair down in the glen must fight their dragons alone."

Somerled, wise soul that he was, agreed.

But he also cast one last meaningful glance at the cliff edge, now almost hidden by thick, curtaining mist.

Devorgilla understood.

"The gloom willnae help them, my little one," she told him, shaking her head. "No glen is hidden enough, no fog so dense, that wickedness willnae find a way.

"So will goodness if certain ill-starred souls trust their hearts."

But for the first time in her long and illustrious career, Devorgilla had doubts.

Gare's heart truly was as dead as he claimed.

Mairi's had been broken beyond repair.

Chapter 2

Gare ducked his head to enter Dunwynde's low-set doorway, astonished that Lady Mairi allowed him the privilege. He'd expected her to walk away, leaving him and Troll in the glen's cold, inhospitable gloaming. Instead, she'd cast a glance at his dog, her face softening before she'd turned back to him with the invitation.

"You're fond of dogs?" He stopped inside the door, allowing his eyes adjust to the broch's dimness.

"I care for all animals." Mairi MacKenzie went to a small table, poured water from a jug into an earthen bowl. "But, aye, I have a special liking for dogs."

"Yet you dinnae have one?" Gare glanced about the humble room, seeing no sign of a pet.

What he did see, hit him like a fist in the gut.

Dunwynde was spotlessly clean, the hard-packed dirt floor, well-swept, while the walls appeared scrubbed and free of moss and cobwebs. But there, all hints of comfort ended. The smoldering peat fire and a few sputtering torches illuminated the circular, windowless room, while a pallet of furs was clearly where Mairi slept.

Gare frowned, rubbing the back of his neck as he took in even more. He doubted the makeshift roof of branches, scraped hides, and heather would keep out a hard rain. Blessedly, the blackened cook-pot on its chain over the fire, and a string of dried herring stretched across the far wall, indicated the lass wasn't hungry. She needn't freeze either, for a woolen cloak hung from a peg near the door. He hoped a lidded basket nearby held more clothes. Even so, a broch was what it was, a centuries-old, long-crumbling stone tower so grim it shouldn't be occupied by more than damp, mice, and the wind-blown scattering of dead leaves.

His mood worsening, Gare felt his hands clench, his chest tighten.

Images of Blackrock Castle flashed across his mind, the sumptuousness of his well-appointed home so at odds to the broch's desolation.

No woman should dwell so sparsely.

That many did, grieved him.

Seeing this one in such straits outraged him, though he couldn't say why her plight affected him so gravely. There was just something about her.

He'd felt it the moment their gazes had met.

"No, I do not have a dog," she said then, setting the water bowl against the far wall. She placed a second dish beside it, a delicious-smelling stew that Troll was already devouring as if Gare never fed him.

"The Glen of Winds is no place for an animal." She turned to face him at last. "There may not be a banshee here, but the souls of the damned do pass this way. Their wails would distress a dog."

Across the room, Troll finished eating, seemingly unaffected by the threat of troubled spirits. Far from it, he went to the low-burning fire, circled three times, and dropped into a deep sleep, his immediate snores proving his ease.

"Troll is no' bothered by your ghosties." Gare frowned at his dog, surprised that he could rest in such a dank, dreary place.

Mairi came over to him, her long raven hair shining in the torchlight. He watched her with interest for he'd heard of the great beauty of MacKenzie women and she proved the truth of their fame. Rarely had he seen such glossy tresses and he surprised himself by feeling a powerful urge to reach out and touch her braid. The thick plait reached to her hips and he was stunned to find he wanted to undo it, see her gleaming hair spill free about her shoulders, an image that stirred him in ways that weren't good for either of them.

She glanced at Troll, then back to him. "Your dog is brave to feel at ease here. I do not fear bogles either, though I do notice oddities. You, sir, are no common journeyer." Her chin came up, her tone challenging. "Why do you carry a broken sword?"

"The rent blade is my penance." Gare told her true. "This sword," – he patted the offensive steel –"is aye at my side, reminding me of deeds that should ne'er have happened, the wrong caused by my hand."

She angled her head, her eyes narrowing slightly. "So that's the reason you're here? You hoped the Glen of Winds banshee could undo an old regret?

"If so I must again disappoint you." She looked at him from beneath thick, sooty lashes. "Just as I cannot restore life to the dead, nor can I change the past. I have no access to the power of the gods, no charms to aid you."

She stood straighter, flipped her braid behind her back. "You shouldn't have listened to the tales."

"I am no fool." Gare leaned toward her. "It was more than that, my lady."

"Such as?"

"A gut feeling. The same instinct that served me well in many a battle. A wise man knows to heed it. Your fame has reached far beyond Kintail. Something compelled me to seek you. I can say no more."

"If you do not, you will not be here past the morrow's dawn." She folded her arms, her spirit intriguing him.

Wishing that weren't so, Gare schooled his features, not wanting her to guess that he found her attractive. More damning, that he'd just imagined her naked, adorned only by her gleaming, unbound hair.

He was beginning to think he'd run mad to come here.

For sure, he wasn't about to tell her of the tiny, black-garbed woman who'd called at his castle gate, pleading weariness and begging a night's lodging. Once she'd supped well and enjoyed her ale, she'd regaled his hall with praise of Mairi MacKenzie. She was a healer of men, a weaver of wonders, the crone had claimed, fixing her gaze so intently on him that he'd believed she'd called at Blackrock for the sole reason of telling him of Mairi.

He half suspected the cailleach had spelled him.

Each time she'd said Mairi Mackenzie's name that night, he'd felt a mighty jolt to the core.

He'd known he had to find Mairi. His surety that she could help him grew with each passing day, every hour. Now that he was here, with her standing before him, he was no longer so certain. Indeed, he had a strong inkling that seeking her had complicated his life in ways he'd never dreamed.

He'd tossed fat onto the fire.

And the flames lured him irresistibly.

Furious at himself, he went to her door and drew back the leather curtain. He looked out into the now-dark night. A thin rain fell and cold mist blew past the broch, the gloom suiting his mood. He let the hanging fall shut again and then rubbed his arms, grateful for Troll, at least, that the lass was giving them a sheltered bed for the night, if only on the cold earthen floor before her hearth stone.

"If you remain silent, you may take your leave now." She appeared at his elbow, a thread of steel in her tone. "Your dog can stay until the rain stops. If you are too far gone by then, I will have one of Sir Marmaduke's men bring him to you. Until then, he shall be kept dry and well-fed.

"If you wish to remain together, you'd best speak plainly." She stepped back then, as if she couldn't bear to stand so close to him.

"Lady Mairi, I lie to no woman." Gare was affronted she'd think so. "I'll no' begin such a despicable trait with you, howe'er you try my patience."

"I am the one awaiting an answer." She crossed her arms, clearly annoyed. "Nor am I a lady. I cannot claim the title, nor do I mind." Her chin came up again, pride glinting in her eyes. "I am simply Mairi MacKenzie. My clan name carries all the honor I need."

"So it does." Gare gave her that.

"You shall have your answers." He moved away from the leather-covered door, feeling as if the night's chill had seeped into his bones, icing his innards, and freezing the words he had to say. It was so hard to push them past his lips. "I am no' here just for myself. My quest serves the weal of every man, woman, and child, of my clan." He paused, closing his eyes for a moment as his gut clenched on the rest. "My journey was also made in the interest of the Scottish crown."

"The crown?" Her eyes widened.

"Better said, the King's Lieutenant, Robert Stewart." Gare's head was beginning to ache. "These are troublesome times, with King David locked away in the Tower of London all these years." He glanced at her, could tell that even sheltered as she was in this wild and remote glen, she'd heard of the sorrowful capture and plight of David de Brus after the disastrous defeat of the Scots at Neville's Cross in northern England, some years before. "Lady," he started again, giving her the courtesy title whether she wished it or not, "my lands, my holding of Blackrock Castle, claim a strategic location on Scotland's northeastern coast."

"Aye?" She lifted a brow.

Gare pulled a hand down over his beard, drew a tight, uncomfortable breath. "I've been served the crown's wish to see me wed. Robert Stewart wants my region secured through an alliance with a neighboring family. The joined might of such a union will strengthen the realm, while the sons born of the marriage will guarantee stability in years to come. If I dinnae comply-"

"Your lands and castle are at risk," she finished for him, sparing him the bile that would've accompanied the words had he said them himself.

"That is the way of it, aye." The admission tasted like cold ash all the same.

He didn't want a wife.

Leastways not Lady Katherine Sinclair, the heiress Robert Stewart's writ suggested he consider. He'd met her but once, at Beltane revels near Aberdeen, finding her shrewish, with a sharp, peppered tongue, and small dark eyes that glinted with malice whenever a fairer, more fetching, maid happened to walk past her, drawing eyes and attention.

Such a woman as a wife would turn a man's life into a misery.

Nae, the Sinclair woman wasn't for him.

But for the sake of his people, he had to find someone suitable. Beatrice Burnett hovered in his mind, being a quiet, unassuming daughter of good house. She'd make any man a biddable bride. Sadly, she'd also bore him into an early grave. There were a few others, though he had no great wish to tie himself to any of them.

By the gods, his inclination was to run from the lot of them.

But that he couldn't do.

So he took another long, deep breath and exhaled slowly, wishing he could rid himself of his woes as easily. That wasn't possible, so he hooked his thumbs in his sword belt and prepared to make his request.

"Fair maid," he spoke true, for she was the most appealing female he'd ever seen, "if not for me, then for my people, I ask your aid. I was told you can weave wonders, even making stones weep and rivers change their courses.

"I ken fine such miracles were bards' embellishments, but no myth or legend is without a seed a truth." He saw her expression changing, becoming shuttered. "I mean no offense, lass. But in all that is said about you, there must be deeds to support your reputation."

She held his gaze, a frown marring her brow. "There are none."

"I dinnae believe you." He went over to her and set his hands on her shoulders, looked down into her great blue eyes. "Mairi MacKenzie, I ask you but one more time. Can you no' find it in your heart to help me?"

She bit her lip as a shiver rippled through her, as if his touch chilled her. "How? To find you a worthy bride? I can promise there aren't any hiding in the rocks and mist of the Glen of Winds."

"I ken the maid I must marry." Gare saw no need to mention Beatrice Burnett's name. "What I need from you is a charm to make me desire her."

~ * ~

"Have you gone addled?"

His fury loosed, Duncan MacKenzie, the Black Stag of Kintail, glanced round the high table of Eilean Creag Castle's great hall, expecting his men to agree. Sir Marmaduke, the flat-footed, ring-tailed recipient of his wrath, merely took another long sip of ale, wholly untroubled.

Everyone else did the same.

Or they poked at their trenchers with their eating knives, cleared throats, and shifted in their seats. Some fussed with nonexistent wrinkles in the table linen. Anything to avoid their laird's eye.

Duncan frowned at them.

No one, not even his own beloved lady wife, Linnet, seemed bothered by the Sassenach's lack of judgment; an error that endangered their clan's dearest, most unfairly maligned cousin, Mairi of the Glen of Winds.

"Sakes!" Duncan turned again to Sir Marmaduke, a man who should've known better, given his long years in the Highlands. As Duncan's friend and brother-in-law, he'd seen how easily treachery could sneak into the most unexpected corners. Mairi's glen was already benighted, ripe for perfidy if not well guarded.

"Your leniency could have dire consequences, English." Duncan set down his ale cup, slapped his hand on the table. "Mairi is alone, trusting us to protect her."

Sir Marmaduke lowered his own cup. "Sir Gare MacTaggert will not harm her." He met Duncan's glare, his battle-scarred face clear and calm as a spring morn. "He carried a broken sword as just Devorgilla foretold. And he came in peace, a good and worthy man."

Duncan harrumphed. "How can you know that?"

"I just did." Sir Marmaduke slid a glance at Linnet. "You above all men should know that there are times when a soul simply knows something. I felt a strange kinship with MacTaggert, my gut telling me it was safe to let him enter the glen unescorted, to seek the maid on his own."

"Say you?" Duncan snatched a flagon of *uisge beatha*, pouring himself a hefty measure, then quaffing the fiery Highland spirits in one throat-burning swig. "I say if any harm comes to her, I will send you back to your bluidy England, minus your addled head."

"Duncan." Linnet placed a hand on his arm, squeezing lightly. "I, too, believe Sir Gare needed to call on Mairi alone."

"You aye side with the Sassenach!" Duncan swiveled about to scowl at his wife. "Or is there something the two of you are no' telling me?"

He cocked a brow, waiting.

Sure enough, the two of them exchanged a look.

"I'm having none of this, be warned!" Duncan gripped the edge of the table and leaned forward, first flashing a glare at his wife, then pinning his friend with another scowl. "Now that Devorgilla's man with a broken sword has a name, we ken he also has a dark past!" He waited, knowing they couldn't argue. "It scarce matters if no man kens why, but he's kept himself holed up in his stronghold these last five years, since the disaster of Neville's Cross. No man turns his back on the world without good reason."

"My friend," Sir Marmaduke spoke in the unruffled tone that aye sawed on Duncan's nerves. "Do you recall when I rode to meet my lady wife so many years ago? You and your lady sent me to her, having arranged our union. I went, and praise the gods I did. On the journey, there wasn't a moment I didn't question if she'd accept me.

"I wasn't just a scarred and ugly brute, but an Englishman, a former knight in service to this realm's greatest foes." He leaned back in his chair, tapping his chin with steepled fingers. "For some reason, Sir Gare struck me as a man suffering a similar plight.

"I cannot say why, but I just knew he needed to meet Mairi, unobserved and on his own." He paused, looking round the table. "As well, I was sure that if danger befell her, he was well able to defend her."

Duncan didn't trust his ears. He felt his face coloring, the flush of anger heating his neck. "Gare MacTaggert left the field at Neville's Cross in disgrace," he reminded his friend. "All Scotsmen there that day, the ones who survived the slaughter, rode away in shame. To his credit, he is said to have stayed when his fellow nobles spurred away, fighting on with the lower ranks, but he's also known to have ne'er raised a sword again, no' since that ill-fated day.

"Why do you think he'd do so for Mairi?" Duncan looked along the table again, not surprised when none of his men took MagTaggert's side.

In the Scottish Highlands, a man who refused to wield a blade was no longer a man.

"I pray he'll have no cause to defend Mairi." Sir Marmaduke took another annoyingly slow sip of ale. "If so, I put my faith in him."

"What you'll do is keep a greater watch on that glen." Duncan stood, needing to pace to cool his temper. "Double your men, hie yourselves out there twice as often, and dinnae hesitate to sweep in if aught appears amiss."

His orders given, Duncan strode from the table. Without a further word or a greeting to anyone else in the hall, he made for an unshuttered window, the one that offered his favorite view, a vista that always soothed him. But this evening, he glared at the shining waters of Loch Duich, the rugged, mist-drenched hills of his beloved Kintail. The gloaming had an eerie cast, causing a strange purplish light to glint off the rocks and water, while the cliffs and headlands on the far side of the loch seemed to stare at him, almost reproachfully.

Duncan rested his hands on the broad window ledge, splaying his fingers across the cold, damp stone. His hills ought to scold the Sassenach, not him.

He only wanted Mairi safe.

He'd sworn to protect her.

"She needs a good man," came a soft voice behind him.

Duncan kept his gaze on the loch. "She needs to live without fear," he answered his wife. Wind wailed past the window then, reminding him of Mairi's glen, and he turned to face Linnet, wishing he hadn't when he saw how the gloaming's odd light made her hair shine and her skin glow, almost as if she were a faery queen.

She was still that alluring, even after so many years.

He desired her fiercely, as a stirring at his groin proved.

Worse, he felt his frown fading, knew a look of total capitulation was stealing across his features. She did that to him, held him aye in thrall. He was helpless to resist her, especially when, as now, she leaned into him, her soft, womanly warmth pressing against him, fuzzing his wits, beguiling him.

"Have done, woman." He heard the roughness in his voice, knew he was lost to her spell. "I only want what's best for the maid."

"That I know, my love." Linnet rose on her toes, kissed his cheek. "I also know that Mairi is not an innocent. You know it, too. Perhaps-"

"Dinnae say you've had another vision?" Duncan hoped not.

"Would that I had." Linnet shook her head, her denial relieving him. "I sense with a woman's kenning" – she stepped back and placed her hand on her heart – "that Mairi is lonely."

Glancing over her shoulder, she lowered her voice. "Her heart has been broken not once, but twice. From what we can guess, Sir Gare has an equally troubled past. I am thinking that mayhap the two-"

"He might lie with her, aye." Duncan could imagine it. Mairi MacKenzie was a beauty, and a passionate woman. "But he'll leave her in sorrow if he does," he added, knowing better than his wife how often landed men bed village women. How easily they walk away.

"I am sure he will not hurt her." Linnet stepped close again, wrapping her arms around him. "Tell Sir Marmaduke to watch the glen, for sure. But make certain the guardsmen stay on the cliffs and do not go down into the glen. No one should disturb Dunwynde."

"You have seen something!" Duncan caught her chin, lifting her face to peer down at her.

"I have not," she denied, the truth in her eyes. "It is only a feeling."

Duncan frowned, certain *feelings* of his own pushing his lovely, ill-starred cousin from his mind.

"I will think on it," he agreed, pulling Linnet close, lowering his head to crush his mouth over hers, kissing her deeply before she could argue.

When she lifted her hands to grip his face, returning his kiss with equal fervor, he scooped her up against his chest and made for a little-used stairwell to the upper floors and their bedchamber.

He'd worry about Mairi and Sir Gare MacTaggert on the morrow.

This night he'd show his lady how much he still desired her. Indeed, he might even take her on one of the landings, so great was his need.

Chapter 3

"A love charm?" Mairi was sure she'd misheard Gare. She also wished his nearness didn't make her feel so startlingly overheated, much warmer than should be possible on such a chill, damp night.

Needing distance, she went to the door curtain, pretending to adjust its ties against the cold, gusting wind. When she turned back to him, she clasped her hands before her. "Is she so onerous then? This woman you will marry?"

"She is no' the problem." He joined her, his long strides easy and commanding, as if he owned the peat-hazed broch. "I have no wish to wed any woman. I haven't for some years."

Mairi blinked.

She needed a moment to grasp the portent of his words. His voice had a deep, richness that made her belly flutter. Her skin tingled beneath his gaze, so she had to struggle to think clearly. When she did, her surprise was great.

"All men wed, especially landed ones of rank." This she knew well.

It was a truth every woman of lesser birth could never forget.

"That may be." He didn't deny it. "Still, a man who is aye away warring can lose interest in hearth and home. His heart hardens."

"You are such a man?"

He nodded. "I am."

Mairi knew color must be blooming on her cheeks. They were so close they might as well be touching. "I am not skilled at healing men's hearts." *I have not been able to protect my own.*

And you have already begun siege.

"Yet I was drawn to your door." He leaned in, his big powerful body stirring her blood, his gaze locking on hers as if he knew. "That cannae be without reason. A man well traveled sees much. He knows there is much in this world that cannae be explained."

"I prefer to try." Mairi glanced at the broken sword he'd propped against the wall. "Seeking answers that satisfy, I mean."

"That's why I am here." His intensity unsettled her, his dark good looks causing a flurry of turmoil inside her. "I seek a way to resolve a problem I can no longer allow, now that the king has cast his eye on me."

"Perhaps you should speak with your wife-to-be?" Mairi tried not to notice how he dominated the broch, his broad shoulders and plaid-draped, mail-covered chest blocking the rest of the small, smoke-hazed room. "She, more than anyone, can give you the succor one needs to ease a heart gone cold. You should have ridden to her."

Something flickered in his dark eyes, a glint she caught because of the torchlight.

He said nothing, his silence hinting that she'd breached a sensitive matter.

"You must be thirsty." She went to her table and poured two measures of ale. His hand brushed hers as he took the cup, the brief touch rippling up her arm, igniting her senses. "I can offer you stew as well." She glanced at the cook pot where her dinner still simmered, delicious steam rising to join the room's peat haze. "Fresh baked bannocks and cheese, a fine herring if that suits you better?"

She gestured to her low, three-legged stool, the only place to sit in the broch. "You can eat there, rest yourself."

He didn't move.

Instead, he took a long, slow sip of ale. "Perhaps later."

He said no more and within moments, excepting his dog's snores, the night wind and the hiss of the fire were the only sounds in the room. It was an uncomfortable quiet, rising to fill the dimness, even as his face shuttered. Mairi knew dark secrets swirled beneath his calm exterior. She sensed it so strongly her heart lurched. Whatever grieved him was a great sorrow.

He was also too attractive, dangerously so.

Especially for her, as she'd been alone so long.

She wasn't the witch the good folk of Drumbell had accused her of being. But perhaps they were right in scolding her as a whore, a fallen woman unable to resist a man's touch. The gods pity her, for she already desired this one's hands on her. She didn't dare look at his mouth too often. As things stood, such hot, potent need crackled between them that she was surprised it wasn't visible.

She was truly her mother's daughter. Born as she was to a too-young, too lusty, village lass who'd given her heart to the wrong man, losing not just her honor, but her life when she'd died birthing Mairi nine months later.

"I'll no' burden my chosen bride with my cares." Gare broke the silence, crossing to the table to help himself to a second cup of ale. "It would no' be fair to her, or any woman, to be tied to a man who'd rather spend his nights before the fire with his dog than entertain a lady wife."

"You do not enjoy women?" Mairi couldn't believe it.

No, she was shocked.

Rarely had she seen a more virile man. Just the way he moved spoke of caged passion, his dark, smoldering gaze marking him as a dangerously alluring man. Leastways for females who appreciated such men.

Women like her, she knew, her quickening pulse proving her folly.

"I cannot believe you have such troubles." She spoke true, her gaze flicking over him from head to toe. "You do not look like the sort of man who-"

"Nor am I." He set down his empty ale cup, started pacing. "I am no' plagued by the *problem* you mean. No' at all, my lady." He shot a look at her, his own gaze raking her, the heat in his eyes proving his words. "I've simply pushed such matters from my mind these past years, in penance. For the same reason I carry a broken sword."

He stopped beside the rent blade, his great physical presence and his proud warrior's bearing so at odds with the sundered weapon.

"There are some deeds that can ne'er be put to right, my lady." He closed his eyes for a moment, pulled a hand down over his face. "When such a burden is heavy enough, all a man can do is quit his debt in other ways. I chose to hermit myself at my home, Blackrock Castle, cutting myself off from pleasures and indulges I'd once enjoyed too greatly."

"Including women, see you?" He started pacing again, a slight flush at his cheekbones showing how difficult it was for him to admit his plight. "My problem is no' an inability to relish a woman, but the almighty guilt that I carry. I am no' sure I can set it aside."

"I see only that you've suffered." Mairi went after him, stopping him with a hand on his arm. "Surely nothing can be so bad to merit such a severe denial?"

He turned, his dark gaze studying her, every slant of his face grim. "And I see why your fame as a miracle healer has spread across the land. You look beyond words and deeds, using your heart to peer into a man's soul. Even so, you err with me, my lady."

His mouth tightened to a hard line as something fierce and terrible flashed across his face. Then he glanced at Troll, his sleeping dog, and his expression cleared. Again, he pulled a hand down over his beard, drew a long, deep breath. When he turned back to her, Mairi knew she was about to hear what truly plagued him.

"I dinnae deserve thon beast's companionship either," he said, the pain in his voice making her heart wince. "But he belonged to someone I loved dearly and so I couldn't abandon him when she died."

"The dead woman is the reason you've monked yourself?" Mairi hadn't meant to speak so plainly.

The words had simply leapt from her tongue, his nearness again disturbing her, his troubles bothering her in ways that weren't wise.

She had her own sorrows.

Caring for a man would only worsen them.

"I am sorry." She stepped back, brushed at her skirts, embarrassed. "I should not pry."

He didn't look offended. "How else can you help me?"

I am not sure that I can. Mairi didn't answer aloud, feeling too badly for him to take his last vestiges of hope. She did go to the narrow wooden shelf on her wall, fetching two plain earthen bowls that she carefully began to fill with stew from her cook pot. She wasn't hungry, but needed to occupy herself, to do anything to keep from standing so closely before him, wanting to take his hand and lead him to her bed, soothing and welcoming him the only way she knew.

Making love to him was exactly what she shouldn't do.

For sure, not when he'd just told her how deeply he mourned a former lover.

"I can help you, sir, by seeing you do not sleep on an empty stomach." She said the only thing she could, placing the bowls on her small somewhat rickety table. "You will eat and then I will make a pallet for you."

She went back over to him and gripped his elbow, leading him to the table where she picked up a spoon and pressed it into his hand. "The stew is not much, but my bannocks are good." She set a basket of them beside his bowl, nodding when he reached for one and took a bite.

"Aye, they are." He finished the bannock quickly, dipping the last bit into his stew. "My sister was fond of bannocks, aye eating more than she should," he told her, helping himself to another.

"She was the woman I spoke of, my sister, Eleanor." He tucked into the stew, his gaze on hers. "She had nothing to do with why I chose to withdraw to Blackrock, shutting myself away from the world. She was simply a wonderful young woman I loved dearly and who left this life too soon. A fever took her, Troll and I were at her side as she went. So now he is mine, and he e'er shall be for I couldn't bear to be parted from him."

"Troll is an unusual name." It was all Mairi could think to say. Mortification blazed inside her, shame that she'd spoken so bluntly, her guess so wrong.

"Why did she call him that?" She ate a bit of stew, hoped the awkwardness would soon pass.

"She didn't. I named him."

"You? Didn't you say he was her dog?"

"Aye, he was." He slid a look at the huge beast, still slumbering beside the fire. "I was the one who found him and Troll seemed a good name for he was living beneath a bridge, snarling and frightening wayfarers, earning the name with his fierceness."

Mairi glanced at the dog, not surprised to see him pushing to his feet and trundling toward them. "He's not fierce now."

"Nor was he then." Gare's face warmed at the dog's approach. "He was injured and starving. The gods only know what happened to him. Had anyone bothered to look, they'd have seen he was hurt and no ravening beast."

Troll reached the table, leaning his bulk into Gare's side. His hopeful gaze and thumping tail left no doubt that he wanted a treat.

Or that he knew he'd receive one.

"He has you well trained." Mairi watched as Gare tore a bannock in two, dipping half into his stew and then offering the tidbit to Troll.

"He is a good friend." He rubbed the dog's ears. "I would have kept him from the start, but he took a liking to Eleanor and wouldn't leave her side. He was her greatest champion. I was away often, so Troll's size and his fearsome reputation kept her safe. She was quite fetching and turned heads where'er she went. She aye saw the good in folk, believing nothing bad of anyone, so it didn't hurt for her to have him with her, always. Troll kens if a soul is pure, or fouled.

"Many were the times he saved Eleanor from grief, his snarls and raised hackles warning if someone meant her harm." He dunked another bannock into his stew, this time giving Troll the entire treat. "He misses her. We all do. She was mistress of Blackrock."

"Ah, so there is another reason you want to marry." Mairi set down her spoon. "It isn't just about chipping the stone casing from your heart, or because the King's Lieutenant has ordered you to take a bride, for the good of the realm. You need someone to run your household."

He raised a brow, his dark eyes narrowing. "Can it be you dinnae like me?"

I am drawn to you in ways that aren't wise. "I do not even know you."

"Be glad that is so." He patted Troll's head, not looking at her.

"I cannot say why, and the fates know I shouldn't care, but I do want to help you." The words slipped from her lips before she could stop them.

Indeed, they'd almost formed themselves.

As if some strange magic had worked a spell on her tongue, making her say things she ought not.

"I am glad." He was still petting his dog, his gaze not on her.

"Then you must tell me who the woman was that put such guilt on you." Mairi couldn't say how she knew, she just did. "If not your sister, then who hurt you so badly that you shun all other women since?"

"She didn't hurt me." He straightened. "I hurt her. She's the reason I broke my sword. The last time I used it, its steel took her life."

~ * ~

Drumbell Village, later the same night.

"So you failed again?" Sorcha Bell stood before her cottage door, her eyes narrowed on the man before her. Once famed for her beauty and charm, and still a great healer, she didn't suffer fools.

An inability to see her will done annoyed her even more.

She waved a hand at the nearby huddle of cottages, where a few cook fires glimmered through door openings and shuttered windows. "I'm thinking you wouldn't have found the wench if she strolled right through Drumbell!"

"My regrets, great lady." The man glanced aside, his gaze on the thin drizzle falling between the great Scots pines that protected the village's far side. When he turned back to Sorcha, he touched his sword hilt and made the sign against evil. "If she was hiding in the cave as we thought, there was no sign of her. No' even cold ash from a cook fire. Naught but some animal dwells there, I swear it."

"Can it be you didn't catch her because she is so pretty?" Anger twisted in Sorcha's gut and she clenched her hands, doubly annoyed because they were gnarled and held age spots. "Men become fools around that one."

"Not I, lady." Her minion shook his head.

"Humph!" Sorcha gave him a fierce look, scarce believing he'd once again been unable to winkle out her arch-rival, the much younger, lust-crazed, and entirely unskilled Mairi MacKenzie. The she-witch who'd been a thorn in her side ever since Mairi's late aunt and uncle brought her to Drumbell as the orphaned get of a whore.

Righteous disdain swelled Sorcha's breast, for she had sprung from much greater stock.

Her father had been a leader of men, captain of the guards to one of the King's most favored nobles, while her mother was renowned for her graciousness and unstinting generosity, her soft-spoken voice said to have been so sweet even the songbirds envied her.

Sorcha hadn't inherited any of her long-dead parents' better qualities.

She did *assume* them.

Quietly pretending that she was just as illustrious, equally admired. In younger days, men appreciated her brown eyes and hair, her small stature, and the soft, pleasing voice she'd learned to pitch like her mother's.

But years had passed and they hadn't been kind.

Even her herb-tending hands had betrayed her for her fingers were now oddly bent, appearing as claws.

It wasn't fair.

Glory such as hers shouldn't fade.

What remained were her healing skills. A gift bestowed on her by the gods, and one that she didn't share gladly. Mairi MacKenzie had grown to be a pebble in Sorcha's shoe. Each time her arch-rival sneezed, a wonder unfolded, bringing her fame and glory. If she blinked or turned her great blue eyes on a man, he fair fell over himself to please her. Even children and dogs had followed her through the village, their gazes adoring. And the elders – Sorcha resisted the urge to spit – they'd looked on her in awe, praising her skills.

It was more than Sorcha could bear.

So she'd taken measures.

To her glee and satisfaction, they'd worked. The MacKenzie wench had been run from the village, barely escaping a fiery end on the stake. A nice stoning beforehand, just to ripen her for the flames, if Sorcha'd had her way.

But someone had warned the chit, allowing her to flee.

No matter, Sorcha wasn't through with her. She had more resources than most knew.

One of them cowered before her now, the big man's hands clutched clumsily, worry stamped hard into his broad, rough-hewn face.

He had reason to fear her.

Sorcha smoothed her skirts and smiled at him, then cast a sly glance at the half-opened door behind her. "This drizzle chills to the bone, eh? You've had a long journey and will be weary. Come in and have a bit of oatcakes and cheese, a horn of warmed mead."

She pushed the door open, letting him see her welcoming fire, the small table with victuals, the great drinking horn on its stand.

"I am hungry," the man admitted, shuffling his feet.

Sorcha's smile deepened, wreathing her aged face. "I've a platter of fine roasted meats as well. You'll sleep with a full stomach."

It was enough.

The man edged past her, ducking to enter the cottage's low-cut door. It was the last thing he did in this life for two of Sorcha's better-trained henchmen fell upon him at once, leaping on him from the shadows on either side of the door. They cut him down so swiftly he'd surely joined the gods before he knew he was dead.

Sorcha nodded appreciation as her men carried him away. Then she made for the wet trees behind her cottage, preferring a walk in the wood to looking on when her minions returned to clean the blood.

She'd come back later, and enjoy her evening meal.

The fine mead she relished.

Then she'd sleep for she needed her rest. On the morrow, she'd take the matter of Mairi MacKenzie in her own hands. She'd had enough of sending fools after the bitch.

This time she'd go herself, and she'd take along men who would not fail her.

Chapter 4

"So, my lady, you have heard the worst of me."

Gare stood beside Mairi's rough-hewn table and beheld a sight he'd hoped never again to see: The blood drain from a woman's face, her eyes filled with horror, the shock of his deed rendering her speechless. His sister Eleanor had reacted the same way, as had the other ladies in his household. Had his mother yet lived, he suspected she would've fainted upon learning what he'd done.

Mairi appeared equally stunned. She'd pressed a hand to her breast, her great blue eyes fixed on his face. "Surely it was an accident," she said, voicing Eleanor's same opinion. "You did not kill her in cold blood."

"How can you know?"

"I just do."

On her words, a gust of wind wailed past the door opening, shaking the leather hanging. From somewhere came the sound of creaking wood and rattling leaves, the glen's birches bending in the wind. The shrieks grew louder, racing round and round the circular broch before they rushed on, having made their presence known.

Mairi glanced at the door curtain, seemingly untroubled by the night's howling gusts. "I feel it here," she said, placing a fisted hand on her heart. "Call it a woman's kenning, whatever you will. It has naught to do with miracle casting or spells. My heart would tell me if you were a murderer."

"The lady is dead, however I am called." Guilt and regret twisted in his gut, terrible memories rising from the blackest corner of his soul. They ripped his heart, reminding him of the grief he'd caused, pain and sorrows that could never be undone. "Her life was spent, cut short by my blade. She bled out in my arms."

"Was it a deed of passion?" Mairi crossed the room to latch back the entry's heavy leather curtain so that cold night air could cleanse the smoky room. "A wife or lover, caught in the arms of another? There are times when one can be so distraught that reason flees."

"I had no such excuse." He didn't lie. "Though I did know her. We'd even been lovers, but only once, many years before."

"I will listen if you wish to speak." Mairi glanced at him from the door, her raven hair gleaming in the torchlight, her beautiful eyes holding no accusations. "It might be good to unburden yourself, whatever happened."

"It is no' pretty tale."

"I have some ugly ones myself." She stepped aside to make room for Troll as he pushed past her into the cold-misted night. "As the banshee of the Glen of Winds, I have seen the worst of men, and some women, including myself, though I have never taken a life."

"I have claimed many, but in war. The exception was Lady Gwendolyn Berry."

She blinked. "A lady?"

"So she was, aye." He joined her at the door, welcoming the chill for the back of his neck felt on fire. Something hard and tight had also lodged in his chest; remorse, guilt, and a wholly unexpected hunger that stirred in him, powerful and dangerous. A fierce urge to yank her into his arms and kiss her long and deep, not stopping until he'd banished the raging ache and emptiness inside him.

"She was English," he said, sure the recounting of the tale would shake him to soul, ridding him of the foolish wish to kiss Mairi MacKenzie. "We met at a champion tournament in France. She was there with her father and brothers. They'd hoped to arrange a good marriage for her, either to a man of rank at the French court, or to one of the attending foreign or English noblemen. I should ne'er have touched her, but she'd caught my eye and so when opportunity arose…"

He let the words trail away, knowing she knew what transpired. "I never saw her again after that night. Indeed, I even forgot her." Guilt stabbed him on that admission, but it was the truth. "I was journeying round the tourney circuit, bold, brash, and full of swagger, enjoying all the attendant pleasures available to such young just-earned-their spurs knights."

"Here, sir." Mairi pressed a cup of warm, spiced ale into his hand, closing his fingers around the offering, urging him to drink.

He hadn't realized she'd left his side.

That she had, and to fetch him such a soothing brew, sent a crack tearing through whatever hard, tightness had settled so uncomfortably in his chest. He could feel it breaking apart, threatening to split wide.

"What happened then?" She watched as he raised the cup to his lips, took a grateful swallow. "When did you see her again? Was it at court? Here in Scotland, or south in-"

"It was in England, aye." Gare tipped back his head, downing the ale. "But we didn't meet at court, and neither at any fine high table in an English stronghold. We clashed at Neville's Cross five years ago, coming face to face during that ill-starred battle."

"She was at the battle, a spectator?" Mairi took the ale cup from his hand, went to pour him another. "I have heard some women travel round with their knightly husbands. Had she wed and was riding with her-"

"She was fighting, in the affray." The horror of the memory rushed Gare, chilling his blood anew. "She wore full armor, sat a caparisoned destrier, and couched a lance as good as any tournament knight. When I first glimpsed her, she was barreling down on me, her spear aimed at my heart, her face and hair hidden beneath her helm."

Mairi gasped, once again looking shocked. "Why would she have been in the battle?"

"I'll ne'er know, no' truly." It was one of his greatest regrets. "She was an excellent rider when I first met her. She'd claimed to have mastered swordery and jousting, skills taught to her by her brothers.

"But I ne'er dreamt to face her in war." Gare shuddered, hoped Mairi hadn't seen. "I did learn that she'd lost a brother and it'd been his gear she'd donned, even his horse and spear."

Mairi stepped closer to the door opening to peer out into the thick, cold mist. Her gaze was on Troll who sat near her peat stack. He'd cocked his head, seemingly entranced by the mist blowing past the broch, the birches at the glen's edge. They tossed in the wind, their silvery branches like raised, waving arms.

"Can it be she wished to avenge someone, her dead brother, a lover or husband?" She turned back to Gare, her brow furrowed as if her next words were difficult. "Or..." She bit her lip, threw another quick look at Troll. "Some women have a wildness in their hearts. Perhaps she did and sought to quench hers by riding into an affray?"

Gare closed his eyes, drew a tight breath.

"There was talk." He wished it wasn't so for he felt, in part, responsible. "Men in taverns and inns spoke of her, a sad tale." He paused, braced a hand against the thick stone edge of the door opening. "I wasnae the only young knight she dallied with at French jousting competitions. Regrettably, she was caught, her name ruined, her family scandalized. They left her there when their party sailed back to England and that was the last I'd heard of her until after Neville's Cross when I made discreet enquiries."

"You cannot blame yourself." Mairi slid an arm around him, leaning into him so that her warmth was a balm to his soul. "Many women have met such fates, lost everything because they were too spirited, giving full rein to their passion."

"That doesnae clear the guilt of the men who helped them into ruin." Gare bowed his head, a muscle jerking in jaw. "A moment's pleasure for a life ruined. It is no good bargain, my lady, and my regrets are deep.

"At the battle, I'd lost my mount and was fighting afoot. That we'd lost was clear, the Scots nobles and most of their captains and best knights had fled the field, but some skirmishes kept on, mostly at the field's edge for too many fallen Scots warriors littered the main battleground. I'd just cut my way out of one of the last smaller routs when a horsed knight charged me, coming at speed and lance couched, ready to run me through. A knight grounded is no match for a mounted opponent – unless, as happened to me, the horse can be brought down and the knight toppled, evening the fight.

"So I grabbed a spear from a slain foot soldier and dropped to one knee, aiming the lance at the charging warhorse." He paused, stepping out into the night's chill damp and tipping back his head to stare up at the dark, racing clouds. "I only needed to wait, see you? The horse couldn't halt his forward rush"

He turned to look at Mairi when she appeared beside him, resting a hand lightly on his arm. "The destrier leapt over a pile of fallen men, then lost his footing, slipping on the blood-slicked ground.

"The beast went down, his rider sailing over his head, straight onto my waiting spearhead." Gare placed a hand over hers, squeezing her fingers before breaking free to pace deeper into the mist, away from the broch. "The cheek pieces of knight's helm flew open at impact and Lady Gwendolyn's shocked eyes stared into mine as she fell, slumping to the red ground, my lance piercing her through.

"She recognized me, I know." He stopped, reaching to rub the back of his neck, wishing it'd been him that had met such an end, not a young woman whose only sin had been her enthusiasm for life.

He waited as Mairi came up to him, the sympathy on her face making it worse. "I saw the recognition flare in her eyes. She couldn't speak, but she stared at me as I eased the helm from her head, needing to be sure it was her - that I'd done the unthinkable and slain an innocent."

"Are you sure it was her?" Mairi's voice was soft and gentle, a beckoning relief in the horror of his memories. "You hadn't seen her in years."

"It was her, beyond doubt." Gare could see the nightmarish scene again now, as clearly as yesterday. "She had unusually light green eyes and a heart-shaped birthmark on her cheek. I knelt beside her, smoothing back her spilled hair to be sure I wasn't mistaken. Her gaze locked on mine, blood trickling from her mouth. Then she was gone, the deed done.

"I broke my sword there and then, vowing to never lift it again." Gare clenched his fists, drew a deep shuddering breath. "When I returned to Blackrock, I did more. I knew I could ne'er again touch a woman."

~ * ~

"You have touched this one." Mairi slid her arms around him, holding tight. She could hardly speak for the thickness in her throat, scarce see his handsome face for the hot, unshed tears stinging her eyes. "No man's sorrow has ever moved me so deeply. I do not have a *love charm* for you, or spelling words to ease your pain, but I can give you comfort and solace for however long it takes to heal your heart."

"I am no' sure I have one, lady." He looked down at her, his dark eyes glinting in the mist and moon-washed darkness. "No' since Neville's Cross, anyway."

"But you do." She rested her cheek on his plaid-and-mail covered chest, hearing his heart's steady thumping. "Everyone does, no matter what happens to us. Yours is only sleeping, waiting for revival."

"Then all will be well." He extracted himself from her embrace, stepping away from her. "For the good people of Blackrock, and for Lady Beatrice Burnett, who shall soon be my bride."

"I am glad." *Your lady shall be the most blessed maid in the land.*

And I shall be the most bereft.

Mairi turned aside, going over to where his dog had plopped down before a bench against the broch wall. She didn't want Gare to see the shimmer of tears in her eyes, to guess that his words had stilled her own heart, dashing ridiculous hopes that he'd kindled inside her. A hot tide of jealousy gripped her, squeezing like an iron fist. Feelings she had no right to, a fierce unjustified sense of possessiveness that was frightening in its intensity.

If she didn't know better, she'd think she was falling in love with the man.

Yet she'd only just met him.

Her heart laughed at the argument, her soul – and old one, she was sure – only smiled, nodding silently, admonishing her for doubting what was true.

Hadn't she known when their gazes first met, that theirs was a meeting unlike any before?

The jolt that had hit her then was proof enough.

But to what end?

He intended to wed another, had sought her aid for that very purpose. She was even helping him, her words this night forging a path he was already following, moving away from her. He'd leave Dunwynde and the Glen of Winds, and return to his own distant stronghold where he'd wed and resume his life with the faceless noblewoman, Lady Beatrice Burnett.

She would remain here, as always on her own with the wind, rocks, and loneliness of the glen.

Only now, unlike ever before, she'd yearn to be elsewhere.

Not at all liking that he'd slipped so easily past her defenses, Mairi dropped onto the little wooden bench beside her door and leaned back against the hard, cold stone of the broch wall. She closed her eyes, furious when she was immediately assailed with images of herself and Gare naked and entwined on the furs of her sleeping pallet. She saw them mad for each other, then flushed and sated from their passionate lovemaking, their hearts pounding with the newfound love neither had thought to find.

A chill ran through her, rippling down her nerves. The pointlessness of her yearning split her heart, making it hard to even breathe.

Gare didn't need help.

She did.

And she didn't know how to begin to fix the ache building inside her.

She was about to push to her feet and go back inside the broch when she heard, "Lady, I have ne'er spoken so fully of that day."

She stood quickly, turning to see Gare striding toward her, his mail and the Thor's hammer amulet at his neck catching the moonlight.

"I still don't understand about Lady Gwendolyn," Mairi said when he stopped before her. *I cannot speak to you about the other one, Lady Beatrice.*

He glanced aside, his gaze on a nearby burn, its surface shining silver through the mist. "There is no' much else to say."

We have more to say than could fill a lifetime. Mairi kept the words silent, waiting as Troll gave a great, noisy yawn. He stretched and then pushed his face against her arm, kissing her hand, before leaving them to disappear into the warmth of the broch.

"He likes you." Gare looked after the dog as he vanished into the broch's shadows. "He aye gave my sister those nichtie-nicht kisses. I have no' seen him show such affection to anyone else."

"He is a good dog." *He is wonderful, and I could love him, too.*

Mary drew her shawl closer about her shoulders, not willing to start down that road. Too much pain and sorrow waited at its end, and each step she'd take along the journey would only break her heart the more.

So she brushed down her skirts, stood straighter, and met Gare's eye, preparing to hear the last bits she needed to push his tragic tale from her mind. "I understand Lady Gwendolyn's fall from grace, as such matters are often called, but whatever made her don a knight's armor and ride into battle, meeting a man's war and risking a warrior's death?

"It doesn't make sense, and" – her heart clenched for the long-dead woman – "I am sorry for her."

"As am I, lady." The bleak look returned to Gare's eyes, his face once more a mask of numb misery. "I meant to tell you. She'd fallen on such hard times that she'd taken to bartering her life for the necks of those knights and soldiers who, for whatever reason, chose not to honor an overlord's call to arms. For coin, she went in their place."

"Oh!" Mairi's eyes rounded. She felt ill.

The poor woman's plight was a worse fate than anything she'd endured.

Nor had she ever heard the like.

"There are men who pay others to fight for them?" As a proud MacKenzie, hailing from a clan forged of Scotland's most valiant and fierce warriors, she could scarce credit any man sinking so low, especially to employ a woman. "You said she was a born horsewoman, had learned to joust like a champion. These are the skills she sold?"

Gare nodded. "I was told she claimed she'd rather die on the field, lance in hand, than in a whore's bed because some lecher gave her the pox."

"Oh, dear..." Mairi's eyed filled and she dashed at her cheeks, her throat thickening again. "A thousand blessings and graces on her soul."

"And on you, my lady." He reached for her hands, linking their fingers when she accepted his grasp. "I thank whate'er powers led me to you. My remorse will ne'er completely fade, nor would I wish it to, given the past. But I now believe I can offer for Lady Beatrice with a clear conscience, certain I will make her a good husband."

"I am glad," Mairi said again, finding no other words.

Those three tasted like cold ash on her tongue, and so suited her mind beautifully. He was squeezing her fingers now, the contact sending currents of sensation up her arms, across her skin and along her nerves. Tingly liquid heat that rushed straight to her heart and poured into deeper, intimate places, damning her.

Her breath hitched and she'd swear the fine hairs on her nape were lifting from the shock. It felt as if she'd snatched a lightning bolt from the sky, closing her fingers around its hot, sizzling core.

Never had a man's touch affected her powerfully.

And he was only holding her hands!

She pulled free, half wondering if he wasn't the one said to cast miracles.

She met his gaze, hoped her voice wouldn't betray her. "Then there is no further reason for you to stay on here." *I wish you would leave now, so swiftly I cannot even draw another breath before the mist closes around you, hiding you from my sight.* "I will prepare a food hamper for you in the morning, enough provender to see you and Troll well beyond Kintail's farthest boundaries."

"You are kind." He was so tall, broad-shouldered, and well-muscled, so ruggedly handsome in the silvery light of so much swirling mist and moon glow. "I will honor your secret here, telling no one that I met you. But this, I promise," he added, taking both her hands again and bringing them to his lips. "I shall ne'er forget you."

"You will leave at first light?" She could hardly speak.

"Aye, you have my word." He nodded, breaking her heart. "I shall pay your respects to your chieftain, Duncan, when I call at Eilean Donan Castle to collect my horse. He should know what a fine kinswoman he has, that I am grateful-"

A great crash came from the broch, the unmistakable toppling of a table, the shattering of earthen cups and bowls, and the loud slurping of a dog eating spilled stew off the hard-packed dirt floor.

"Troll!" Gare sprinted into the broch, calling to his dog.

Mairi followed more slowly, needing to gather her wits. She was almost glad the beast had made such a mess, knocking over the table to steal the remaining stew in their dinner bowls, the untouched cheese and her famed bannocks. Cleaning up after him would keep her occupied, giving her something to do besides make a pallet for Gare.

She wasn't sure she could bear that.

Not knowing that once he'd slept there, he'd leave her forever.

Dunwynde and the Glen of Winds banshee forgotten and wiped from his mind, no matter how much he swore that he would always remember her.

She knew better.

Much as she wished she didn't.

Chapter 5

"Troll!" Gare skidded to a halt inside the broch's devastated main room. In truth, the ancient ruin's only room. He set his hands on his hips, frowned at his dog. "Have you gone daft, laddie? Did the lass no' give you a well-filled stew bowl of your own?"

The dog looked back at him, licking his lips as he did so, his canine gaze unblinking.

Guileless, he dropped his huge haunches in the middle of the mess from Mairi's toppled table. One leg had broken. The two earthen bowls that had held his and Mairi's supper were cracked in halves, the useless shards cleaned of any stew that might have clung to their sides. Nary a speck of food littered the well-swept floor, making clear that Troll had gobbled all evidence of his mischief, save the pool of spilled ale that was slowly spreading. The ale cups were intact, but the jug was shattered beyond repair.

Blessedly, the night wind had extinguished the table candle when Mairi latched back the entry's leather curtain or a worse disaster might have greeted them.

As things stood, Gare felt terrible.

"My apologies, ne'er has he done anything the like." He turned to her for she was still behind him, in the doorway. He was stunned to see her smiling.

Troll barked and lumbered over to her, pressing his bulk into her legs.

The fiend's tail swished, his lolling tongue almost making him look proud of his handiwork.

"It's no bother." Mairi turned her smile on the dog, reaching down to ruffle his ears. "He was hungry, no more."

Gare rubbed the back of his neck, frowning. "He broke your table," he said, glancing at the rickety piece that was already a disgrace.

Stooping, he picked up the shattered leg and tossed it on the room's central hearthstone. It caught fire at once, the flames bright and blue-orange, crackling loudly as the wood quickly burned.

"I'll repair the table before I leave," he offered, wishing he could do more. He turned back to Mairi, his scowl worsening to see that she'd dropped to her knees beside his dog and had wrapped one arm around Troll's massive shoulders. She appeared to whisper soft words into the beast's ear. "My regrets that doing so will delay our departure," he added, noting Troll's sly, one-eyed sly glance.

"It shouldn't take long." He'd make certain. "We can be away before gloaming."

"As you wish." Mairi didn't look at him, her attention on Troll who'd stretched out at her feet, freeing his furry belly for rubs. "Perhaps we can roll in one of the larger rocks, jam it beneath the table?"

She looked at him then, her suggestion spearing his heart. "Such would serve well."

"Nae, it willnae." Gare was outraged.

"I wouldn't mind." She stroked Troll's chest, scratched beneath his chin. "As long as the table doesn't wobble, it will be fine."

"You shouldnae be eating at such a crude table at all." His opinion came more harshly then he'd intended, but she unraveled his wits, made him think and behave in ways that were so unlike him he scarce knew himself since he'd entered her windy, rockbound glen.

"Truth is," - he stalked over to tower above her and his dog – "I cannae believe a man like Duncan MacKenzie would allow his kinswoman to sit at such a poor excuse for a table. Aye, he disappoints me."

"He isn't to blame." She spoke quietly, pushing to her feet and smoothing her skirts as he met his irritated gaze. "My laird would've carted all the luxuries of Eilean Creag Castle to Dunwynde had I allowed him. We even argued about it, but his lady wife took my side."

Gare looked at her, more confounded than ever. "She wished you to live so poorly?"

"Nae." She shook her head. "She wished me to live."

Moving away from Troll, she re-latched the door hanging, then dusted her hands. "Lady Linnet agreed with me that a procession of comfortable furnishings being transported clear across Kintail would've drawn attention. My reason for being in this glen was and remains that no one knows I am here.

"The goods in this broch," - she gestured round at the meager household – "all came from a small shepherd's hut in the next glen. Everything you see was brought over the hills or along low-lying burn channels either at night or under cover of dark, fog-drenched days."

"I see." Gare did, much as he didn't care for her needing such precautions.

An equally great concern was why her plight troubled him so.

"I see you do like dogs." He sought a safer topic as he moved to help her straighten Troll's mess, for she'd begun gathering the shards of her broken earthenware. "Most ladies would no' be so tolerant of such antics."

"I told you I have a heart for dogs," she said, dropping a bowl half into the small wicker basket she held. "Troll reminds me of one I had at my home, Drumbell village. I loved him dearly and ache for him still."

She bent to pick up another bit of broken pottery. "I lost him less than a year ago. His name was Clyde, for he was found there as puppy, abandoned on the banks of the River Clyde, just outside the great city of Glasgow. A wandering family of no clan ties passed through Drumbell, staying for a few nights, telling tales and playing pipes and fiddles in exchange for pallets, ale, and meals.

"When they left, they forgot Clyde." She paused, drew a deep breath, swiped at her cheek. "I do miss him."

"He looked like Troll?"

"He did, very much." She glanced at the dog, her eyes suspiciously bright, her voice catching.

Gare felt like an arse.

He wasn't actually sure why, but he did. He also felt other things and it was becoming harder and harder to ignore them. Worse, he wasn't sure he wanted to.

"I am sorry, lady." Closing the short space between them, he drew her into his arms, holding her close, wanting only to comfort her.

"So am I..." She didn't finish, leaning into him so that he felt a tremor ripple through her.

"I cannae think of losing Troll." He ran his hands up and down her sides, settling them on her shoulders, tightening his grip just enough to soothe her. He hoped. Unfortunately, feeling her warm softness pressed against him was a pleasure he hadn't known in so long. Even more disturbing, he didn't just feel her lush, pliant body crushed to his, he had the oddest sense that she was somehow becoming a part of him. As if her heart and soul were flowing into him, melding with his to leave an indelible imprint on him.

A branding, a claiming, he suspected would remain. And not just for the duration of his journey home to Blackrock, but all his living days.

"It is hard to lose a good friend." He drew her closer, resting his cheek against the crown of her sleek, raven hair as he slid a glance at Troll.

The great hairy lump ignored him, his eyes tightly shut as he gave a loud, fluting snore. It was a noise so painfully fake that Gare would've thrown back his head and roared with laughter under any other circumstances.

As things stood...

Sons of Odin, he was kissing Mairi's brow!

Gare straightened at once, releasing her as if she'd turned into a grizzly-chinned, wart-nosed crone. He hoped to the gods she hadn't noticed the kiss. It was bad enough that he had, the warm silk of her skin still haunting his lips, the fresh clean scent of her hair playing havoc with his senses, stirring his manhood.

Across the room, Troll rolled onto his side, craftily showing them his back and treating them to more phony snores, giving them privacy.

Gare shoved a hand through his hair, sure he'd run mad.

He was also doomed.

He'd sought Mairi MacKenzie hoping she would work her magick so that he could cast the shackles from his heart, so he'd make Lady Beatrice a good and worthy husband.

Now, gods help him, he had a new reason not to want to marry the Burnett heiress.

One he couldn't consider.

~ * ~

"Clyde is the reason I am here." Mairi chose her words carefully, hoping her tone didn't reveal that his unthinking kiss to her brow had unsettled her so greatly.

"Your dog?" He'd started pacing, but stopped now, turning to look at her. He sounded puzzled.

She wasn't surprised. "In a way he brought me to this place, aye. Like as not, I'd still be at Drumbell if he hadn't died."

Uncomfortable beneath his gaze, she placed the basket of broken pottery beside the door and then took a heather broom from the shadows, proceeding to sweep her floor. She needed to busy herself, a task to occupy her hands lest they reach for him, trying to claim what she had no right to desire so fiercely.

"It was Clyde's loss that turned the villagers of Drumbell against me." She risked a glance at the big warrior, her breath catching to see he'd removed his plaid and was pulling off his mail shirt.

Praise the powers, he'd sought a darkened corner to do so, and that he'd turned his back. She didn't want to see his naked chest, hoped he'd not strip down beyond the tunic she knew he'd be wearing beneath the mail.

"It was known how much I loved the dog." She spoke quickly now, nerves making her rush. "Some claimed that if I had the gift everyone believed I could've worked a wonder to keep my pet alive.

"But he was old, it was his time." She brushed along the wall's edge, not really seeing what she was doing for the heat swimming in her eyes. It'd been long since she'd spoken of Clyde. It hurt to do so. Yet for some reason, she wanted this man to know how things stood with her. Why she'd come to this bleak, sequestered place.

She glance at him again, found he was frowning at Troll. He'd folded and placed his plaid atop one of the baskets that held her clothes, and his steel-linked hauberk glimmered on the floor beside the basket.

Blessedly, he still wore his tunic.

The linen shirt hugged his powerful muscles, showing her every hard-hewn muscle of his chest and arms. She swallowed, wishing she hadn't seen, but torchlight threw flickering shadows on the wall behind him, limning his strapping body, the pale light leaving no secrets. His broken sword was propped nearby, the halved blade reminding her why he was here, and of fates worse than hers.

But the dance of light and shadow also spilled across her bed of furs, and seeing him standing so close to her sleeping place made her pulse quicken, despite the grim truths she meant to tell him.

She wanted him badly, gods help her.

She tore her gaze away before he caught her looking at him. It was madness to do so. Everything about him proved a danger for her. She could even see a dusting of dark hair shadowed beneath the tunic's cloth and her fingers ached to trace the arrowing pattern from his chest lower, straight down to his groin. Her blood heated, her belly fluttering. Determined to squelch such thoughts, she plied the broom with renewed vigor, whisking around the smooth rocks that circled her hearthstone, then moving on to poke the heather branches at the three legs of her stool.

If need be, she'd sweep all night, even cleaning the lower reaches of the broch's circular walls.

"It was cruel for anyone to scold you for no' saving a dog you loved." Gare's voice came from across the room. He sounded angry, which didn't surprise her.

He was clearly a good man.

A landed noble, a chieftain and great warlord who cared about honor and believed that no one, whatever their station or what they may have done, should be treated unjustly.

Lady Beatrice Burnett was a lucky woman.

Mairi resented her greatly, which made her less goodly than her guest.

Sure her desire for him was earning her a place in hell, she raised the broom and took a few hefty swats at the leather door-curtain.

"I would have done anything to keep Clyde alive, given all I had, though the gods know it wasn't much." She could hardly see now, took blind swipes at the hanging. "My cottage at Drumbell was small, only slightly larger than this broch, though I'd taken care to make it a cozy and comfortable home. It was mine, inherited from my late aunt and uncle who raised me. Even loving my home as I did, especially my garden, I'd have surrendered it gladly to help Clyde.

"But there was nothing I could do." She felt chilled, hard memories making her heart pound wildly. "I had no bat toes or newt's eyes to mix into a potion for Clyde's achy hips, no magical herb to restore his labored breathing. No powers to cast a miracle." She paused, drew a long shaky breath. "I've told you I am as ordinary as anyone else, certainly unable to bring the dead back to life, or keep an old and weary dog from dying.

"You will have done what you could." The rasp of a buckle warned that he was removing his sword belt.

"I did." She closed her eyes, willed them to stop leaking.

Behind her, a dull *thunk* on the floor proved she'd guessed correctly about his belt. Her eyes snapped open, but she wasn't about to turn around.

"Voices were raised against me, fingers pointed." She moved down the wall, gripping the broom tighter, swishing the heather branches at nothing. "Many railed that I'd deceived them, that I'd boasted of powers I didn't have. Yet I'd always argued the opposite, insisting I was only a village lass, capable of no more than knowing the right herbs to brew a tisane for a sore throat, or a sleeping draught.

"I tended my garden for a love of green, growing things. The feel of good, damp earth beneath my fingers, and the loamy richness I loved to breathe in." She blinked hard, not wanting to swipe at her eyes again. "I enjoyed the harvest, sharing its bounty, helping those in need if I could." She pressed a hand to her breast, inhaled deep. "Never did I use my garden to craft spells or harm folk."

"That I know, lady." He spoke again from the other side of the broch, his voice tight, even roughened.

"They called me a witch, saying Clyde had been my helpmate and without him, I was nothing. That I'd lost my powers with his death." She stopped, setting the broom against the wall so she could dab her eyes with the edge of her shawl. "They wanted to stone and burn me. They-"

"They were fools."

Mairi swung around, surprised to find him right behind her. How had he crossed the room so silently? For such a big, tall man, he moved with the devil's own stealth. He also looked as dangerous.

"Lackwits the lot of them, and you, lady, are anything but ordinary. You are a prize beyond telling." He pulled her into his arms, crushing her against him as he rained a storm of kisses on her face and her throat. Then he groaned and slanted his mouth over hers, thrusting his tongue inside and kissing her almost savagely.

Mairi clung to him, sliding her arms up and around him, gripping his broad, strong shoulders as she welcomed the onslaught. She twined her fingers in his hair, drawing him closer, her entire body melting when she felt the hard ridge of his arousal nudging her belly. Even through their clothes, she could feel the heat of him, the corresponding warmth at the center of her crying out to know him intimately.

It was madness.

Yet she couldn't stop kissing him, feared she'd die if he tore his lips from hers.

Some crazed, wild-hearted part of her wanted to beg him to choose her, to forget Lady Beatrice and be hers. Staying with her at Dunwynde or taking her with him wherever he wished to go. As long as they heeded the powerful pull between them, she didn't care.

Never had she been so roused from a mere kiss. Yet Gare kissed her unlike any other man she'd ever known. He devoured and drank of her, branding his passion on her as surely as if he'd seared his name across her heart. Her entire body quivered, the longing for more almost unbearable. He kissed as she'd known he would the moment she first saw him, and worse, as if he'd already claimed her lips a thousand times or more, and was only coming home.

That rightness terrified her, knowing he'd leave on the morrow.

She started to pull back, but he broke away first, his breath coming hard and fast. He shoved his hands through his hair, the look on his face a knife in her heart.

"By the powers, lass, I didnae mean for that to happen." He stared at her, shaking his head as if he couldn't believe what had come over him.

"My apologies." He sounded sincere, but distant, as if he'd already pushed her from his heart. "I cannae say what came o'er me. There is just something about you. My wits are scattered since entering this glen. I am no' myself here." He paused, once again shaking his head. "It willnae happen again, you have my word."

"It was only a kiss." *You branded me for all my days, perhaps beyond.* "No harm came of it, and I enjoyed it, so you needn't worry you shocked or tainted me." Lifting her chin, she met his gaze, her own as proud as she could make it. "I've told you that I am not a lady. What I am is a woman and I have known a man's touch. My blood runs thick and strong, and I am not shamed by passion."

"You are a great lady, Mairi MacKenzie." His voice was deep, still roughened by their kiss. "Any man would be proud to call you his own."

I do not want any man. I wanted you.

She bestowed her coolest smile on him, prayed to all the gods, those known to her and any she hadn't yet heard of, that he couldn't see how she was breaking inside, bleeding from the heart, her soul weeping.

She'd loved before, or thought she had. Twice, if she counted her young husband-to-be, a fine farm lad taken from her by death before they could speak their vows. And her more recent lover, a lying, conniving sixth son of an impoverished knight who'd abandoned her to wed, the daughter of a well-pursed Inverness merchant.

Now she questioned how she'd felt about either.

For regardless of Gare not wanting her, no matter what the emotion inside her truly was, she'd never known such a powerful, all-consuming draw to someone. It went beyond craving, yearning, and desire.

How foolish to think she could hold him so tightly that he wouldn't be able to let go?

That he wouldn't want to?

That their kiss had slammed into him with the same ferocity as it had her.

"You, sir, should be glad we kissed so heatedly." She flipped back her braid, silently thanking her every MacKenzie forebear for the steel in her backbone, the strength in her heart. "There can now be no doubt that Lady Beatrice will be a most pleasured bride."

"Lass…" His voice held a note of sorrow, the anguish saying either how much he regretted kissing her, or that he longed to do so again, but wouldn't.

She couldn't tell.

When he didn't move, made no attempt to reach for her, the answer was clear.

So be it.

Mairi hitched her skirts and brushed past him, going to a broad stone ledge on the wall where she kept a store of uisge beatha. She poured two measures, knocking back her own with a swiftness that would've made her chieftain proud. She carried Gare's portion across the room, her chin high as she handed him the small cup.

"Drink, and then take your night's rest," she said, nodding as he tossed back the fiery spirits. "I want you gone before the morning light burns away the last of the glen mist."

Turning, she went to her three storage baskets and lifted the lid on the largest, retrieving several clean, neatly folded woolen blankets. She placed two on another basket, and then shook out one, intending to spread it on the floor near the hearthstone.

But Gare was already at the door, his plaid draped over an arm.

"You needn't make me a pallet, Mairi MacKenzie," he said, guessing her intent. "I'll sleep outside your door, wrapped in my plaid."

"Wait, it's a cold night, and the mist is damp..." She started forward, ridiculous guilt sluicing her. But he'd already stepped out into the darkness, the door's leather curtain falling shut behind him.

Mairi sank onto the floor, only realizing that she'd sat beside his dog when the great furry beast stirred, resting his head in her lap.

He resumed snoring at once, falling back into a deep canine sleep, and seeming so comfortable she couldn't bear to disturb him.

Nor did she want to, for Troll had also stolen his way into her heart.

"Oh, dear." She took a deep shuddery breath, gently stroked the scruffy fur between the dog's ears. "Whatever am I going to do, Troll?"

He didn't answer.

Though she would've sworn he cracked an eye, giving her a quick look of great satisfaction.

Chapter 6

"That should do you well, my lady." Gare watched Mairi carefully as he stepped back from the repaired table, looking to see if even the slightest change of expression flickered across her cool, closed face. But there was nothing. Only the same distant politeness she'd shown him since sunrise, when he'd collected an ax from her to fell a good, sturdy branch from the nearby birch wood.

"I am grateful." She nodded, her gaze on the new table leg. "It was good of you to fix it."

"I'd have preferred oak, but the table stands steady. It willnae tilt when you use it." He wanted to see her at his high table at Blackrock, claiming pride of place beside him at that huge, magnificently crafted masterpiece, the as yet unoccupied lady-of-the-castle's chair just as richly engraved and beautiful.

He felt a muscle jerk in his jaw.

She shouldn't eat at rough-planked cast-off from a shepherd's hut.

Worse, he hated that the repaired table would always remind her of their ill-fated meeting. The mad, wild and wondrous kiss they'd shared. A kiss that had carved deep wounds into the souls and hearts of them both, he knew. He could see the pain all over her, in her eyes, her cool, shuttered face, and in the overly polite tone of her voice.

She loathed him.

And she had every reason.

She'd gone to the broch's door where the leather curtain was latched back, giving a fine view down the whole of the narrow, steep-side glen. "The mist will be lifting soon."

"So it will." Gare followed her gaze, speaking as levelly as he could. "Troll and I will be away anon. I gave you my word."

She inclined her head again, her glossy black braid slipping over her shoulder to hang to her waist. "I am glad you remember."

"I aye keep my word." He did, even when it didn't please him.

Feeling that way now, he stared past her into the glen, too aware of the temptation she presented. He felt a fierce urge to undo her braid, to let her gleaming black hair stream across the back of his hand, spill through his fingers. His need was so great, so strong, he didn't dare look at her.

The glen was safer.

It beckoned as the start of his journey home. He couldn't wait much longer either.

It wasn't a sun-bright morning, but enough light slanted through the clouds to chase the chill mist and drizzle that usually blew through the Glen of Winds. For two pins, he would've sworn the gods were conspiring against him, snatching away the mist tendrils at speed, their anger at him so great that they stole his last excuse to stay on in the sweet, soothing, and powerfully seductive presence of a raven-haired, sapphire-eyed vixen named Mairi MacKenzie.

A woman he had no right to have touched, much less kissed.

Gods help him, he wanted more.

He burned to scoop her into his arms, carry her to her bed of furs, toss up her skirts and spread her legs, showing her with all his passion and need how much he desired her. Far gone as he was, he'd also bare his heart to her, confess that he'd never felt so strongly for another woman in all his life. That he suspected he could, or perhaps already was falling in love with her. He did know he wanted her safe and that he couldn't stand the thought of leaving her in this empty, rockbound gorge.

In truth, Kintail's highest peaks hugged the valley floor so tightly, the Glen of Winds could hardly be called a glen.

For a crazy-mad moment, he considered telling her that he wished to show her true glens. The broad sweeping beauties that filled Scotland's vast northeast where he made his home.

She'd love Blackrock, he was sure.

But he said nothing.

Lady Beatrice Burnett's quiet face hovered before him, as did Robert Stewart's writ. The parchment damned him, its wax seal and the bold, slashing signature of the King's Lieutenant – and his own - making it impossible for him to heed his heart, to abandon plans forged to safeguard Scotland's oft-times most troublesome and perilous territories.

With privilege came duty, and he'd sworn oaths to uphold his.

Feeling despicable, however untarnished his knightly honor, he glanced to where Troll had slept away the morning beside Mairi's peat fire.

His good friend wasn't there now.

And his bowl of morning stew hadn't been touched.

Gare frowned, pulled on his beard. Troll ate well and with gusto, never missing a meal. He was also not shy about begging for more. There could be no good reason for the dog's lack of appetite.

"Have you seen Troll?" He joined Mairi at the door where she'd already placed a bulky linen sack of victuals for his leave-taking. "He was there by your fire last I looked and he hasn't eaten his breakfast."

"I saw." She glanced at the bowl, piled so high with beefy stew. "I thought he doesn't care to eat so early in the day.

"Troll would ne'er stop eating if I allowed. He doesnae care when he eats, only that he does."

"Clyde was the same." Her face softened, the sadness in her eyes, spearing Gare's heart.

"I am sorry you lost him." He was, and he didn't know what else to say.

He wanted to touch her cheek, tuck that stray hair behind her ear, then cradle her face in his hands and kiss her again, long, deep, and slowly this time. It was a need that hardened him at once, his unchained desire for her making clear how urgently he needed to be gone.

"Any guess where he's gone?" he asked again, glancing into the broch's shadows.

Changing the direction of his mind before his need became obvious.

"Nae." She stepped back, drawing her shawl closer about her shoulders, putting distance between them. "Perhaps he needed to go out?"

The word 'go' apparently drew him, for Troll appeared at once, coming through the door opening without a glance for either of them. He also ignored his food, walking past the bowl to the farthest, darkest corner of the broch where he circled three times and then plopped onto the cold, earthen floor, clearly wanting to sleep.

Gare frowned when a chorus of bogus snores ensued.

His friend was up to something, and it wasn't any good.

The dog also turned his massive shoulders to them, his great head facing the wall. Rarely had Troll been so courteous. He hardly ever gave Gare privacy, most times sticking to his side like a burr to wool.

"There is something amiss with him." Gare crossed his arms, thinking.

They had a long trek before them. Duncan MacKenzie's Eilean Creag Castle, a stronghold on the other side of Kintail, stood nearly to the Isle of Skye. Great, rocky peaks raged between, an arduous journey for beast and man. Even huge and strong as Troll was, he'd tired quickly if they set off with Troll not having eaten.

"It's no' like him to ignore food." Gare turned back to Mairi, himself ready to run a hundred heather miles naked and starving just to be far from her. The ravening hunger she stirred in him, the almighty attraction he felt for her. "Have you aught else he can have before we go? I'm thinking he ate so much stew last night, he's after something else. Aye, that'll be the way of it."

"Could be..." She glanced at Troll, began tapping her chin. "I do have some sliced roasted capon. It's good, plump meat if he'll eat it."

"That will do." Gare nodded. "Troll loves chicken, any way it's prepared. Perhaps you can spare a bit for our journey?" He didn't like asking, but Troll's behavior concerned him. "He'd surely be glad for it, however much you can do without."

"I'll fetch it now." She moved away, the emptiness she left behind hitting him like a fist to the gut – even though she'd only crossed the room.

"Sweet lady," he called after her, the endearment leaping from his tongue, his words having a will of their own, speaking without his consent. "I'd ask a boon for myself, if you'll allow me?"

She turned back to him, a small packet of roasted capon slices in her hand. "I would deny you nothing," she said, her gaze solemn. "You may take anything of mine that you desire, if you chose to ask."

She stood straight, her sapphire eyes blazing into his, seeing everything he was sure. Her words, the double meaning of them, set him like granite. Indeed, he wanted her fiercely. Never had a woman affected him so powerfully.

And with only a few words and a direct look from her knowing eyes.

Gare drew a tight breath, everything in him straining, ready to break. "When we spoke last night," he finally managed, giving voice to the other need that plagued him, the one he could address in honor, "you didnae say why the talk of your powers started? All legends and myths have a seed of truth.

"Before I leave, I'd hear why folk bestowed you with such claims." *Tell me true, and quickly. If you dinnae, my other need will win and I will grab you to me, damning us both.*

"It is a sad tale." She placed the capon on her table, clasped her hands before her. "I will share it if the telling interests you."

"It does." Gare thanked the gods she didn't come forward, that she remained across the room.

She smiled, but it was a distant smile, and fleeting. "Let me first pour you ale, for it may take some time for me to finish."

So she did, filling not one cup, but two. And outside, the sun burned away the last few curls of mist, bathing the glen in cold autumn light.

~ * ~

"Come walk with me. I'd rather not speak of such things in the broch's shadows." Mairi stepped past him into the morning, leaving him no choice but to follow if he wished to hear her tale.

It was a cold, brisk autumn day and the wind wailed through the glen as always. But the sky held patches of blue and the burn sparkled brightly, as if some great hand had cast diamonds across the clear, rushing water. The many rocks seemed to smile at her, greeting her as the friends she'd come to think of them. Even the tinkle of the burn was a joy, like the laughter of faeries, caught in a sunbeam.

For all the bleakness around her, she loved the Glen of Winds, and felt a deep attachment. How sad that she'd leave here for the man coming after her, yet he would shun such a sacrifice, returning alone to his Blackrock Castle.

She stopped beside the burn, the rush of the water calming her.

Faery magick.

Or just the cold, clean wind off the falls.

Most says such things soothed her. But now only one man lingered in her mind. She could think of nothing else.

Any moment he would reach her, his long-strided steps bringing him to her across the rocky, broken ground. Then he was there, stopping beside her, his face wary as he glanced about her sanctuary.

"The mist is gone," he said, voicing what she knew.

"So it is." She slid a glance at him, a grievous error.

He was staring at the far end of the glen, his gaze on the shining waters of one of the waterfalls that gushed down the higher cliffs. The glen's shrieking winds dampened the roar of the falls, but it was clear that he was awed, that he appreciated the splendor.

Would he look at her so raptly?

If she were to disrobe here and now and offer him everything she had?

Don't leave. Not yet. Give me a chance to make you mine.

"You see why I don't mind being here." She reached out and stroked his arm, letting her fingertips glide over his arm rings, drawing his attention. Touching him was the one thing she shouldn't do, but she couldn't help herself. "If I had to leave Drumbell, this is a good place."

"It is no' fine place for a woman alone." He turned to her, gripping her elbows. "I am troubled to know you here."

"It is a better refuge than anywhere else." She lifted a hand, held her hair against the wind. "The souls of the doomed do race through here. I have heard and seen them, I know they are real. Many fear them, so most will not come this way.

"That dread keeps me safe." She held his gaze, wanting to remember his face, every line and angle. How his dark hair caught the light, the strands shining in the sun. "Folk will mourn lost loved ones, but few want to meet their spirits."

"Yet there isn't a banshee?"

"Not that I'm aware." She studied the sensual slant of his mouth, how the morning sun also touched his beard, making it glisten. "Perhaps there was such a washer woman here, long ago?" She glanced aside at the rushing burn. "This would be a good place for a banshee to wash the bloodied shirts of those marked to die, to wail and moan in sorrow for them."

"I would hear of you, no' this glen and its legends." He touched her cheek, lifting her chin with one finger. "What started the tales that you have the power to bring the dead back to life?"

"Because I did." Mairi told him plain.

"So it is true?" Something flickered in his eyes. "I'd thought you must have special gifts. You are a maid like no other I have known."

"I have told you, I am not a maid." She adjusted her shawl, felt a prickle of ill ease. She didn't want to disappoint him. Not because she was a woman of passion, no longer pure. But because she could tell he suspected she'd used an enchantment to snare his desire.

That he wanted her stood clear.

Hadn't she felt the hard ridge of his arousal when he'd kissed her?

She had, no mistaking.

As he was leaving, she doubted that she'd be confronted again by his rock-solid need, however much she might wish otherwise. So she'd do what remained, and speak honestly.

"Just as I am village born and not of higher blood, nor does a witchy magick run in my veins." She drew a deep breath, her love for the aunt and uncle who'd raised her shoring up her pride, steeling her backbone.

She stepped away from him, went to the burn's edge. "What happened had nothing to do with wonders or a miracle. It was years ago at a Lughnasadh harvest fair. I was walking past the food stalls, trying to decide what I wanted for my lunch. A wee lad was eating a meat pie when he choked. He'd gone red, his eyes streaming as he fell to the ground, unable to breathe.

"I was closest to him, so I grabbed him into my arms, clutching him tight as I ran about, searching for his parents." She looked down into the burn's clear water, seeing the scene again. "They came rushing up to me as I pressed him to my chest."

She looked up then, not surprised to find Gare beside her. "Perhaps it was more the gods not wanting to claim such a young soul, than anything I'd done. Whatever the reason, before I could release my grip, he stirred in my arms, coughing loudly and then gulping great breaths of air, his life returned"

"I can see why folk would credit you with miracles, especially at a Lughnasadh fair where the old gods are honored, ancient magick in the air." He stepped closer, stroked her hair back from her face. "In truth, folk were right to laud you for saving the lad."

"I am glad I was there." She was. She'd do the same again, even knowing how the deed would change her life. "That winter, something else happened. A small loch at Drumbell had frozen and villagers were using bone skates to glide across the ice. It cracked and a girl fell in, disappearing into the freezing water. She was pulled out, but it took too long and by then it was clear she'd drowned.

"The lads who'd drawn her from the loch placed her on their plaids at the water's edge and I was fetched, folk believing I could bring her back to life."

Mairi shivered and rubbed her arms against the chill spreading inside her. For sure, she'd aided an innocent young girl that day, but it was also the deed that brought her the wrath of Sorcha Bell.

"What did you do?" Gare's dark gaze slid over her, something in the way he was looking at her making her fear she'd break when he left the glen. "I see no sorceress before me, but a beautiful woman with an open, generous heart. The folk in your village should have honored you."

"Oh, they did." She couldn't keep the bitterness from her voice. "For whatever reason, I somehow revived the drowned girl. Perhaps she wasn't truly gone? I'll never know. I can only tell you that I acted on instinct, pure fear for her life and a burning wish to aid her. I knelt beside her, listening for a heartbeat, feeling for her pulse, but there was none. Her skin was cold and blue. She wasn't breathing so I set my hands on her breast, pushing hard, again and again, trying to force her lungs to work.

"They didn't, so I leaned down and blew my own breath inside her, thinking that perhaps my breath would sustain her, make her again pull in her own. She did, her eyes popping open as she gasped and sputtered." She paused, another great chill flashing down her spine. "Around us, the good folk of Drumbeg cheered, crying with joy for the lass, praising me as a wonder healer.

"I have never seen such jubilation." She hadn't, though at the time she'd never guessed the ramifications. "One soul stood apart, glaring at me with such venom that the heat of her hatred scorched my bones."

Mairi's stomach roiled with remembering. "She was the village hen wife, a healer of great renown in those parts. Her name was Sorcha Bell. She'd never liked me, never cared for another healer who might earn more praise and respect. She resented others who worked with herbs and potions, understood the old ways and the power of the moon.

"And that day…" She paused, shuddering. "I'd knew made her a mortal enemy."

"She is why you became the Glen of Winds banshee?" The fierce look on Gare's face said he already knew.

Mairi nodded anyway. "She had a vicious temper. It annoyed her when villagers called at my cottage, asking for herbs from my garden, a salve or healing tisane. After the lad at the harvest fair and the lass in winter, her resentment worsened. She claimed I was the devil's bride.

"Then when I lost Clyde..." She didn't finish, the words snagging in her throat, her eyes burning. "I told you what happened. She turned the village against me. I fled Drumbell and have been here since. Perhaps I should have stayed and faced her, but I am yet young, and" – she lifted her chin, barely seeing his face for the shimmer of tears – "I am passionate, see you? I wanted to live."

"Sweet lass..." His eyes darkened then and he reached to cradle her face, lowering his head. "You are more than passionate and-"

"No more kisses." Mairi raised both hands, holding them before her as she backed away. "The mist will roll in again when the light starts to fade from the sky. I want to be alone when that happens. I'm asking you to leave now."

He frowned, but made no move to come after her. "Is that truly your wish?"

"It is." *Never. Come with me to the broch. Lie in my arms on my bed of furs.*

Be mine forever.

"So be it." He nodded, his face grim. "I will fetch Troll and we'll be on our way."

"I thank you." Mairi's heart stammered.

But it didn't matter. All that did was that Gare and his dog left as swiftly as possible and that they kept a good pace over the hills. She wanted them faraway by gloaming, so distant that they wouldn't hear her weeping.

Her cries for them to return.

Chapter 7

Gare stopped outside Dunwynde, letting Mairi enter before him. The walk from the burn had opened his eyes, showing him why he'd reached for her, the reason he'd almost kissed her again. It wasn't Mairi MacKenzie who'd spelled him. The strong emotions thrumming in his veins had nothing to do with how she'd melted into him when he'd held her. Nor was it the way she'd run her hands up his arms and over his shoulders, clutching him with such stunning female need.

None of that had aught to do with the power of feelings raging inside him.

It was this place.

The Glen of Winds.

So much savage grandeur played havoc with a man's soul, quickening his blood. For sure, the hills around Blackrock were also grand, the great mist-drenched peaks even mightier, their mass impressive enough to stir any man's heart. But he'd scarce ventured beyond his stronghold in recent years, a sequestering that made him apprcciate the Glen of Winds' splendor more than he would've otherwise.

He wasn't sure.

He just knew the thunder of falls and the sun glinting on the burn affected him. On the higher ground, the mauve and purple of heather gleamed in the clear autumn light, while the ever-present wind carried the earthy-sweet scent of Mairi's peat fire.

What man wouldn't reach for a bonnie lass on such a fine, luminous morn?

His urge to kiss her had nothing to do with her great blue eyes or how the slanting sunlight limned her with gold, drawing attention to the fine womanly shape of her, or the sheen of her raven hair.

Gare's heart hammered. He sent another glance down the glen, his pulse quickening even now as his gaze moved over the sheer crags and rushing cataracts, the wind-tossed birches along the glen's high rock-sided edges.

No man could deny such glory.

And when had he become so adept at spinning fables?

All the splendors of Scotland paled beside the woman who'd just slipped into the shadows of the half-ruined broch.

The glen hadn't made him want to kiss her.

She had.

And she'd entranced him with much more than her sweetly turned ankles and the gloss of her hair. He wanted her in ways he'd never desired another woman. A truth that didn't surprise him because she was, after all, unlike every other female he'd ever known.

Gare heaved a great sigh, heard the wind picking up, whistling through the trees. He'd promised to leave by gloaming. Now he wished he was already gone, well over the hills and away.

He'd go at once, putting distance between them before his heart overrode reason.

At a brisk pace, he could be at Eilean Creag Castle by nightfall. He'd toss Troll over his shoulder and carry the beast if he wearied.

He only needed to fetch Troll.

Before he could, Mairi appeared in the broch's doorway.

"Troll hasn't still eaten." She glanced over her shoulder, looking worried.

"That cannae be." Gare stepped past her into the broch, scarce able to see in the dimness after the morning's bright light.

Even so, Troll's great bulk was unmistakable, sprawled so listlessly beside the broch's central fire. Only a few steps away, his large bowl of stew winked from beside the wall, the contents piled as high as ever. Cold, congealed, and wholly untouched.

"He's ne'er gone so long without eating." Gare frowned at the dog, not surprised that his eyes glowed demonic red in the firelight.

For sure, he was up to something.

Too bad, Gare was having none of it. He wouldn't be outfoxed by a dog.

"I dinnae believe he's ill." Nae, he *knew* he wasn't.

Ailing dogs didn't wear sly expressions.

"I don't know…" Mairi bit her lip. "It's never good when an animal doesn't eat."

Nae, it isnae. But no' for the reasons you're thinking.

"Do you still have the roasted capon from earlier?" Gare remembered the treat she'd retrieved. "Or is it already packed with the other provender?"

"It's here." She went to the table, the new birch leg gleaming silver in the dimness. She indicated the cloth-wrapped package, opened now to display the succulent breast slices within.

"I've been trying to hand feed him, but he only turns his head away, refusing even a bite." She took a small piece, went to kneel beside Troll. "Here, laddic," she offered, holding it out to him. "Just a wee taste for me, please? Only one and I'll leave you be."

Troll didn't blink.

Nor did he turn his big furry face away from her outstretched hand.

He pinned a look on Gare and gave the most pitiful moan to ever cross his doggie lips. Then he rolled onto his side, showing them his back.

"He must be ill." Mairi left the capon tidbit on the floor beside Troll's head and straightened, dusting her hands. "Clyde stopped eating, too, not long before-"

"He will eat anon, I promise you." Gare shot an annoyed look at the dog, not surprised to see an ear twitch.

The beast knew they were talking about him.

"If he doesn't, I'll put him on a barley water and gruel diet when we return to Blackrock." Gare kept his eye on the dog as he spoke. He was rewarded by another ear twitch, this time accompanied by a flickering of the dog's closed eyelids.

Troll didn't care for his threat.

"Indeed," – Gare hooked his thumbs in his sword belt – "perhaps we'll forget the gruel, and just give him barley water.

"Until he's feeling himself," he added, waiting.

Another pitiful moan filled the broch, a deep sorrowful sigh.

"He has been drinking." Mairi crossed the room to peer at Troll's water bowl.

"Then he'll have enough strength to cross the hills." Gare was sure of it.

He glanced at the provender sack Mairi had filled for them. It still sat by the door. But for some reason, he couldn't make himself reach down and sling it across his shoulder.

He knew why, and the reason infuriated him.

He should never have touched Mairi MacKenzie.

It'd been madness to kiss her.

It was equally daft to stand here now, with her crossing the smoke-hazed broch, coming right up to him.

"You should eat something, too." Her gaze slid over him, slow and assessing. "The hills between here and Eilean Creag are trackless, the going rough. You'll journey better with sustenance."

Before he could argue, she took his arm and drew him to the table, set with oatcakes, cheese, and a tray of smoked herring. Her touch lit his skin, sending heat straight to his groin. Worse, something in his chest unfurled, a strange and curious sensation.

A feeling he'd never known and didn't want to embrace now.

He willed it away, pretending he hadn't noticed.

"Lady, you are kind." He took the oatcake she offered, and a small bit of cheese. "I will partake gladly."

He was a doomed man, after all.

"What are your plans?" She stepped back from the table, leaving him to help himself. "Once you've reached Eilean Creag."

"Duncan MacKenzie will surely offer me a night's lodging, and then I'll collect Rune, my horse, and be away." He glanced at her, immediately wishing he hadn't.

Her great blue eyes were fixed on him and his heart leapt just looking at her. For a beat, he couldn't think straight. When he could, something in her gaze hinted that she felt the same odd awareness that crackled between them, and that only made things worse. He tore his gaze away, reached for another oatcake and a herring.

"I'll thank your chief and his men for granting me passage across their lands, especially into this glen." *I won't tell them I now wish I'd ne'er come here.*

"Lady Linnet enjoys guests. Her hospitality is praised throughout the Highlands." Mairi spoke from the door, her back to the smoky room. "She'll try to keep you there, leastways for a few nights."

"Then she will be disappointed for I must return to Blackrock at haste." *If I remain in Kintail any longer, I'll ne'er leave, or I'll be taking you with me when I go.* "I have much to do along the way home. Most importantly, I shall call at Burnett Tower near Inverness," he added, putting the dread task in words.

So he couldn't ignore the deed.

His sworn duty to his king and the realm. The good people of Blackrock, who relied on him.

He didn't touch his food, his stomach clenching. "I must speak with Lady Beatrice's father, make arrangements to-"

"Marry his daughter," Mairi finished for him, her voice as cool and level as her back was straight.

"That is the way of it, aye." Something inside him broke on the admission. It was a terrible fiery twisting, a rift of jagged misery deep in his chest.

He went to stand behind her, placed his hands on her shoulders, his chin atop her head. "I am sorry," he said, hoping she'd understand his meaning without forcing him to say words that would only hurt her. Rip his own soul into a thousand or more pieces.

"The King's Lieutenant has my oath." It was true. "The very day I set off on my journey to find you, I sent his courier south with my sworn agreement to do the crown's will, securing a strong alliance for the northeast – through marriage to a fellow chieftain's daughter.

"Such an oath is binding." Gare fisted his hands on her shoulders, wished he couldn't feel the reaction rippling through her.

He closed his eyes, drew a long, deep breath. How ironic that he'd come to the Glen of Winds in the hope its banshee would release his heart from the hard stone casing that had built around it.

Instead, he'd learned there wasn't a banshee, but a beautiful, desirable woman.

Rather than freeing his heart so he could love another, she'd claimed it for herself.

~ * ~

"I will also speak to MacKenzie about you." He turned her to face him, gripping her elbows as he looked down at her. His face was hard-set, his gaze fierce. "Your safety concerns me. I dinnae care to think of you here alone. You'd be better off at Eilean Creag. It's a formidable holding, guarded not just by the loch surrounding its isle-girt walls, but a garrison of Scotland's most famed fighting men, warriors led by a man who's already a legend."

Mairi almost smiled, and would have if her heart weren't breaking.

Duncan had pressed her with those very arguments when she'd first called at his door, asking for sanctuary.

He hadn't claimed to be legend, but he was.

All men knew it.

"The Black Stag would agree, for he made me those very arguments himself." She wouldn't lie. "But if you knew my clan, you'd know there's no race more thrawn. MacKenzie women are even more stubborn than our men, so you'd both have no luck dragging me from this glen.

"I told him then that I'll not be responsible for drawing the wrath of Sorcha Bell on Eilean Creag and my kinfolk who dwell there." She turned back to door opening, the day outside still clear with autumn light. "She's a formidable foe and she'd shy at nothing to harm me." She paused, rubbing her arms as a chill raced through her. "She'd also not hesitate to attack anyone who'd help me."

"All the more reason you should heed your laird's will and let him protect you within his castle walls. He is a great man, he-" He broke off, sounding frustrated.

He braced a hand on the door's edge, lowered his head to stare down at the threshold's stone slab. "MacKenzie is known to protect his kin. He will keep you safe. Let him."

"He does." Mairi returned to the broch's deeper shadows. It was hard to have him so near, yet already so far removed from her. She didn't want him to see the shimmer of tears in her eyes when he left. "The men he sends to guard the glen are his best. Sir Marmaduke is his own good-brother and a champion swordsman."

She stopped beside her fire, extending her hands to the glowing peat bricks. She needed the warmth for a terrible cold was spreading inside her. "There are other ways I'm protected."

"Aye, the spirits of the damned." Gare sounded even more annoyed. Proving it, he threw a scowl at Troll. "Bogles didnae keep me from entering this glen. I cannae be the only man in Scotland no' afraid of ghosts."

He straightened then and came to her with three long strides. He gripped her shoulders, looking fierce. So tall, strong, and magnificent that her heart almost wept. "Heed me, lass, for I've seen the worst of men." His voice was rough, his dark gaze piercing. "Myth and legend will only work so long, then-"

"I didn't mean the spirits." Mairi stiffened. She knew what spurred his concern. He wanted to ride to Lady Beatrice without guilt and worry plaguing him. "Lady Linnet is a *taibhsear*. Her gift of second sight is even greater than most seers because she is the seventh sister of a seventh sister."

She lifted her chin, met his gaze levelly. "I cannot recall her ever erring."

"I cannae see how her gift would aid you." A muscle leapt in his jaw. "Men and a stout curtain wall-"

"She'd sense any danger that might approach the glen. My chief trusts in her and would act to would protect me. So you see, I am well guarded on all fronts. You can leave without a care." She back straight, her voice strong. "MacKenzies look after their own."

"They must also sleep." He slid another look at Troll, then turned away to shove both hands through his hair. "I'm of a mind to take you with me to Eilean Creag, leaving you there."

"I would not go." She wouldn't.

She did fold her arms, hoped he'd be away soon. Her stomach was knotting. Dread coiled deep inside her, the knowledge that when he and his dog left the glen, disappearing up the cliff path, she'd never see either again.

"I am not your concern." She moved away, brushed at her skirts. "You can put me from your thoughts as soon as you've climbed the track out of the Glen of Winds."

"You are no' a maid easily forgotten, Mairi MacKenzie."

"I must be for you to call me a maid." *Did I not tell you I am no such innocent?*

He flashed her a dark look before snatching a piece of roast capon off the table and striding over to his dog. He dropped to one knee beside the beast, his broad back to her as he held the treat before Troll's slumbering nose. "Lady, if you've spent as much time as I have at court and on the tourney circuits, you'd know that a woman's true innocence dwells in her heart, no' betwixt her legs.

"Forgive the harsh words," – he glanced at her over his shoulder – "but they must be said. Any man who'd turn away from you because of something you've done in the past, is a man no' worthy of you."

Mairi blinked, not knowing what to say.

Nor could she have spoken if she wished because a hot thickness was rising in her throat.

"Your chief should arrange a marriage for you." He poked Troll's mouth with the roasted meat, scowling even more when the dog wakened and turned his great head to the side, shunning the food.

"He did once." Mairi found her tongue, long ago hurts, and a love she'd always cherish, helping her to speak past her sorrow. She clasped her hands before her, waiting as Gare grumbled to his dog and then pushed to his feet, leaving the treat beside Troll.

"My mother died birthing me and I never knew my father," she began, wanting him to understand. "I was raised by my aunt and uncle. They were village farmers, famed only for the size and tastiness of the onions that grew in their garden. My uncle did a fair trade at markets in Kintail and elsewhere in the Highlands. Duncan MacKenzie arranged for him to sell his onions to an innkeeper on the Isle of Skye.

"The inn was on the harbor at Kyleakin, so was well-visited." She began pacing, memories swirling from the darkest corners of her soul. "I sometimes accompanied my uncle when he delivered his onions to the inn, and so-"

"You caught his eye?"

"Not the innkeeper's, but his son's," she explained. "His name was Patrick for his mother was Irish."

A peat brick on the hearthstone popped then, sending a shower of red-orange sparks into the air. Going to the fire, Mairi took her poker and nudged at the mound of peats until they again simmered quietly.

"He was a big, strapping lad with laughing eyes and a wicked smile." She drew a breath, long ago images pinching her heart. "I was young, had never been in love, not even kissed..."

"Until this lad pursued you." Gare was leaning against the table with his arms crossed, his gaze on the glowing peats. His dark hair gleamed in the firelight, his tall, warrior's body so out of place in the small, smoky room. He was simply too magnificent, should be striking such a pose against the marbled hearth of a great noble's finest solar.

Like as not, his Blackrock Castle held such luxuries.

And wasn't that a good reason for her to ignore how the air around him seemed so charged with his powerful presence? The bold and potent virility and strength that drew her so irresistibly that she was sure her femininity sang just to breathe the same air.

She shouldn't feel such fierce longing.

She bit her lip, willing her need to cease.

"He paid me court, aye." She lifted her braid, toyed with its end. "He made me smile and laugh, he wrote songs for me as he fancied himself a bit of a poet. He won my young heart, which I gave him freely."

"I regret nothing." She spoke the truth in her heart. "If I could turn back the years, I'd not want to miss our brief time together."

"MacKenzie offered terms for you, suggesting a marriage?" Gare spoke then, his gaze locked on hers. "He arranged the betrothal and the lad left you?"

Mairi nodded. "So it was, but Patrick didn't leave me because he didn't want me. He did, and we spent stolen hours indulging our youthful passion in Kyleakin's hidden corners – trysts that made me a woman.

"Then, just as the betrothal was to be finalized, he died." She closed her eyes, the memory still painful. "He'd been waiting for me high in the hills above the harbor when a storm hit. My father wouldn't allow me to leave the inn, and so Patrick waited. By the time he realized I wasn't coming that day, the storm had turned fierce.

"The hills are steep thereabouts, the ground strewn with rocks, some loose." Mairi began to pace, speaking quickly before her throat could close again. "He slipped on the muddied ground and fell to his death, striking his head as he hurtled down the cliff, landing in the sea."

She turned at the far end of the broch, meaning to pace back to the door, but Gare was right behind her, blocking the way.

"By the powers, lass." He reached out and took her hands, squeezing her fingers. Nothing but sympathy stood on his face and seeing it broke her heart anew.

Not for Patrick, but for knowing what a wonderful husband Gare would make. She hoped Lady Beatrice was worthy of him, but she also wished the woman didn't exist.

Guilt now joining her sorrow, she held Gare's gaze. "It was long ago."

He gripped her hands tighter. "I am sorry, lass. Such a loss will have been hard for you, especially so young."

"It was, and I will never forget him."

"Nor should you." He released her hands to slide his arms around her, drawing her close. "You do the lad honor, and that is good."

"There was another..." She hadn't meant to speak of her more recent lover, but Gare's embrace unsettled her, causing the words to spill free. "He was a traveling smithy, journeying about to ply his trade. We met and so" – she felt the heat rising in his cheeks, annoyance beating through her – "he stayed on in Drumbell, courting me and making plans for a life together, once he'd saved enough coin to start a family.

"I should not have believed him." She knew that to her cost. "But I was so lonely, see you? He was a fine looking man, and lusty. He drew the admiration of all women, from wee girls to crones, for he had an easy way of speaking, turning phrases that made any woman feel special, as if he saw only her, and was enchanted.

"What he saw was opportunity." Mairi lifted her chin, hot bile flavoring the words. "I allowed him to sleep at my cottage and he supped at my table. I washed his clothes and stitched repairs as needed. Then a fat-pursed Inverness merchant stopped at the village when his horse had thrown a shoe. As the work was done, the merchant spoke of Inverness's need for well-skilled smithies. He also told of his beautiful daughters, the hefty bride prices they'd bring."

"The smith left with him?"

"The next morn. I was a fool."

"Nae, you were a woman of passion. You *are* one, the gods be praised." He cupped her face in his hands, his gaze fierce. "You are a treasure and will make a fine wife someday."

His words were the ones she'd most dreaded.

A truth she had to face.

Knowing now was the time, she went to the door. The light was fading, the sun low and dim behind the darkening clouds. There was also a hint of rain in the air, and mist clung to the highest peaks.

Gloaming was nigh, and Gare was still here.

A part of her rejoiced, the rest of her quaked with the awareness of what the night would bring.

If it rained, she wouldn't let him sleep outside.

If he stayed with her...

"I am sorry, lass." He came up behind her, putting his hands on her shoulders. "I meant to leave earlier. I can still go now. I'll carry Troll if need be. He-"

"Nae." Mairi shook her head, preparing herself to do the only thing she could: Claim what little bit of him that she could, so she'd have something to cherish once he'd gone.

"It is too late." *You cannot cross the hills in darkness and my heart cares too much to let you.* "I will make us a warm supper and you can depart on the morrow." She looked out into the glen, its steep, rockbound edges hazed now by soft shades of blue and gray.

The smell of rain was stronger, coming on the raw, wet wind.

"If it rains, you can sleep in the broch," she said, aware she was sealing her fate. "There is room before the fire." *My bed of furs will keep you warmer.*

"You are sure?" He slid his hands down her arms, resting them at her hips. "I've no' wish to trouble you."

"You won't." She leaned back into him, inhaling his scent. "I want you to stay."

Before he could answer, the sun slipped behind the hills, the glen darkened, and the winds picked up, bringing the first splatters of rain.

Chapter 8

A full sennight later, Gare eased back Dunwynde's door flap and frowned into the cold, wet night. He also struck his fist against the saturated stone of the door's thick-cut edge. Mist and sideways rain blew everywhere, and the howling wind could indeed pass for the wails of the doomed – or the cries of a banshee. Rarely had he seen such downpours, surely not lasting a full seven days. Not since his tourney years, so long ago, in so many strange lands with equally odd weather.

Yet when a cloud sailed from the moon, revealing the glen's tall, rain-slicked walls and dark, wet birches, he knew exactly where he was.

Mairi's Glen of Winds.

Still.

His mood worsening, he dashed the water from his face, half ready to believe Mairi held the ear of the weather gods. Or that his besotted dog had taken her side in Gare's quandary. He could see the beast championing his favorite with his best interference and stalling skills.

Troll knew his mind.

He was also greatly adept at cajoling others into his corner.

He'd always preferred the lasses. Not that Gare could fault him for that.

He did frown at the meddlesome beast as he slinked back from the nearest outcrop, so drenched that he looked like a dripping denizen of the sea. For sure, he didn't resemble the once-ferocious battle dog of a long-forgotten warrior.

He was simply Troll the Terrible.

Gare knew his tricks.

He'd heard the dog creep from his plaid beside the fire, had watched his slow, hinky-hipped gait as Troll nudged aside the door's leather curtain. Then he'd surprised Gare by loping easily to the nearby tumble of stones. He'd run without any sign of pain, as if he had nary a care in the world.

He'd faked his limp these past seven days.

Gare had a good notion why.

Troll wasn't pleased that he hadn't joined Mairi on her bed of furs.

Gare wasn't happy about that either, but he preferred the pain of restraint now to a lifetime of regret later. The price of touching her was too high, the cost, too crushing to Mairi. His feelings scarce mattered, but he wouldn't break her heart.

He was acting nobly.

Doing what was best from them both.

He just never would've believed that keeping an oath would make him feel more like an arse than a valiant.

So he drew a tight breath, narrowing his eyes on Troll as he trotted closer. If his dog thought he was a fool for not touching Mairi, he could be excused because he knew nothing of the importance of honor, a man's sworn word, and the duty that comes with privilege. A King's writ is binding, irrevocably blessing or damning a man, however the crown's wishes happened to fall.

Never had he broken a pledge.

He wouldn't now.

Even if walking away from Mairi would snuff out every last glimmer of the light she'd restored to his life.

"So you knew?" came her soft voice at his elbow.

"That his limp vanishes when he goes out?" Gare glanced at Mairi, stroked the hair back from her face, unable not to touch her. "I ken as of this night, aye. I suspect his miracle happens only when he believes no one is watching him."

"There's more you don't know." She sent him a quick smile, stepping back so Troll could shuffle inside, once again assuming his achy-hipped gait.

"Watch out." Gare grabbed her arm and pulled her out of the way just as Troll stopped near the fire to shake his great dripping bulk. Soot, ash, and peat smoke rose in a gray, cough-inducing cloud that drifted everywhere.

He threw a glare at Troll, sure the bugger was laughing.

"I shouldn't be surprised, scoundrel that he is." He turned back to Mairi, releasing her. "Had I no' grabbed you, we'd be covered in soot."

"But we aren't, and the mess is soon righted. My broom will sweep it away and the rain will freshen the air." She glanced at Troll, a smile dimpling her cheek as the dog circled thrice and gingerly lowered himself onto his sleeping plaid. "Some might say Troll is mightily clever."

"That he is." *I'd wager my beard that he hoped to see me no' just grab, but kiss you.*

Praise the gods, a good warrior kept his wits at all times – even men who carry broken swords.

"So! That was no great task." Mairi returned the heather broom to its place against the wall. His broken sword was propped nearby. The polished blade and the broom's heather presented an unmatched pair, shouting their different stations.

No matter.

She had a smile that pierced his soul and warmed his heart, proving how little he cared.

"What else did the beast do?" He didn't really want to know.

"We can be glad of this one." She tilted her head and glanced at Troll, now sprawled before the fire. "The lad's not ill and he hasn't lost his appetite. He just hasn't been eating from the food bowl here."

"Is there another?"

"Not inside the broch." She kept her gaze on the dog, a corner of her mouth lifting. "He's been sneaking the food I set out for the glen's wild creatures. There's a wee red fox, almost tame and very smart, with remarkably knowing eyes. Then the usual squirrels, rabbits, martens, and a colony of wildcats."

She shrugged, her face softening. "More red deer than I can count."

"You feed them all?" Gare frowned, not surprised. His mind whirled. As he was beginning to know Mairi MacKenzie, she'd do just that, even setting out her own last supplies so her four-legged friends didn't hunger.

She laughed, a rich, velvety laugh that did terrible things to the hard knot she'd put into his chest.

"Aye, I feed them all." Her smile grew as she set her hands on her hips and cast another glance at Troll, who was watching her with slit-eyed stealth. "And because you are so much like my liege, I know why you're asking.

"The Black Stag also worried I'd not have enough for myself." She went to a darker area of the broch and came back with a large bowl that she placed where rain dripped through the roof thatch, forming a puddle on the hard-packed earth floor. "Now whenever Sir Marmaduke and his men make their rounds, they bring sacks of leftover viands from Eilean Creag and fill the troughs. The men cut pine shoots and grasses for the deer, also bringing acorns and nuts. The troughs are in the wood behind the outcrop.

"Troll must've smelled the food." Gare paced, rubbing the back of his neck. "I am glad he's no' ill, that he's eating. But we should've been away days ago."

"He is a fine dog. He surely had his reasons for wanting to keep you here a bit longer."

Gare set his jaw, sure that was true.

He just wished he could do more than admire Troll's choice in ladies.

But his hands were tied, his word given.

And inside Dunwynde on such a cold, wet night, beside Mairi MacKenzie's peat fire, all he could see was the luminosity of her creamy skin, the blueness of her great sapphire eyes, and her luscious lips that he knew were so soft and warm.

Just looking at her sent need racing downward so that he had to turn away, not wanting her to see how much he desired her.

As if she knew, she appeared before him. "I know you'll ask why I didn't tell you I saw what Troll was doing," she said, placing her hand on his arm. "I couldn't because I knew what you'd do when you found out."

"Indeed?" He arched a brow. Her light touch affected him too much to say more. If he tried, he might blurt that all he wanted was to join her on her bed of furs and ravish her.

"Aye." She nodded. "I believe you have a bit of a temper. Not so bad as Duncan MacKenzie in a rage, but strong enough that you might've taken off with Troll. I worried you'd traipse across the hills in the teeming rain.

"You could've fallen ill, both of you." She glanced at the sleeping dog. "Troll may not be sick now." She leaned in, her voice low. "He would've caught a chill had you gone.

"So I meant to tell you after the rains." She went to her bed of furs, turning back the top coverlet as she did each night before sleeping.

It was a signal for Gare to retreat to the far side of the broch and his makeshift pallet.

The hour for him to no longer look her way – he had once and so was aware that she slept naked. Damn his eternal soul for peeking! He'd also made it his habit, once settled in his own bracken-stuffed pallet, to turn his eye on the space between the doorjamb and the leather curtain.

Old ways died hard.

Especially for champion knights.

And so it came that he caught a flash of silver in the rainy dark. A drawn blade carried by a great hulk of a man with a broad, hard face, and loathing in his eyes. His thick beard was hung with several small bones and he'd thrown a bear skin around his shoulders. He looked like a Viking warrior from darker ages and was surely as brutal. Gare watched as he reached the base of the cliff path, where moonlight glinted off his sword and shone on his bone-hung beard.

Then he was in shadow again, disappearing behind the outcrop.

It didn't matter.

He'd been seen.

Gare knew from his quick glimpse at the assailant, that he was just that.

He also knew why the brute was here.

He was coming for Mairi.

~ * ~

"Sorcha sent him."

Mairi lifted on her toes, leaning close to whisper into Gare's ear. "He's here to kill me."

"He's here to die." Gare whipped around, just as she was about to say more.

Their lips brushed.

A jolt raced through her and his expression turned fierce, hinting he'd felt it, too. Stepping back as if she'd scorched him, he ran both hands through his hair and glanced about the broch, his gaze searching the shadows.

"I should've kept the ax in here and no' in your byre." He threw a furious look at his broken sword, her own weapon so dull-edged it would scarce cut peat. "No' matter. You'll stay here with thon blade of yours and Troll at the door. I'll sneak round before he leaves the cover of the outcrop. I cannae fetch the ax fast enough, but if I charge him from behind, surprise will work for me.

"He'll no' expect a man with you." His voice was harsh, his face grim-set.

Mairi's heart thundered. "You'll be killed." She glanced at the door. "Leave now, take Troll. While you can."

Looking more fierce than ever, he grabbed her to him, kissing her hard and swift, before releasing her as quickly. "The time for me to leave was the moment our eyes met. 'Tis now too late."

"All the more reason I'll not see you die." Mairi touched his face, slid her fingers across his beard. She'd think later about the implication of his words. "Sorcha follows a dark path. She spells those beard-bones and mumbles incantations to make the wearer invincible."

"No man is that." He crushed her to him again, squeezing tight. "There's a greater power than her ancient evil."

Troll was already at the door, pacing. His hackles were raised and low growls rumbled in his chest. Mairi knew he'd defend her to the end – if Sorcha's man killed Gare.

"Stay at the back of the broch, tip over the cauldron if need be." The look he gave her was fierce, commanding. "The bastard could slip on the muddied floor, giving you a chance to flee."

Mairi nodded, fear and dread sweeping her, making her lightheaded.

She knew what Gare meant by 'if need be.' The possibility chilled her to the bone. She started to say so, but he lifted the door flap and disappeared into the cold, blowing rain.

"By all the mercies, I never wanted this!" Ignoring his order, she ran to the door and dropped to her knees beside Troll. She wrapped an arm around the dog, pulling him close. "I'm so sorry, laddie. I know you love him." *So do I...*

Leaning forward, she pressed an eye to the slight space between the leather curtain and the door's edge. She saw only rain and the glen's great peaks, so dark under the roiling clouds.

Sorcha's man and Gare were nowhere to be seen.

Then Troll's hackles rose even more and his snarls deepened. In the same moment, the huge, bearskin-cloaked assailant strode from the birches into the glen, making no attempt to conceal himself.

He was heading for Dunwynde.

He'd gone only a few paces when Gare burst from the trees, charging after him. Mairi clapped a hand to her mouth, looking on in horror as Gare flew into the brute, roaring a challenge as they both slammed to the ground.

Mairi ran outside just as the assailant's sword flew from his hand. Gare leapt off him with lightning speed, snatching the blade and swinging it in a fast down-slashing arc that could've disemboweled an ox. Equally fast, the big man jumped to his feet, bellowing as he yanked a huge double-bladed war ax from a sling across his back.

Troll was frantic, running circles around her, barking loudly.

Mairi pressed her hands to her face and stared at the two men, scarce feeling the wind and rain.

"So she's returned to her whoring ways!" The big man tossed the ax into the air, smirking as he caught the spinning weapon by its haft. He flicked a glance over Gare, clearly assessing his strength and skill as he demonstrated his own prowess by twirling the ax in an array of dizzyingly fast curves. "Shame to carve up a good warrior and noble," he taunted Gare, not looking sorry at all. "I'll be glad for your dog. I'm in need of one!"

He pointed the ax at Troll. "Thon battle dogs are well-loved in my folk's northern home!"

Not blinking, Gare tossed his sword high into the air, catching its hilt with the same ease as the assailant and his Norse ax. "That is good," he returned the challenge. "You may search for such a dog tonight - in the mead halls of Valhalla!"

"Nae." The man shook his head, his gaze flicking to Gare's hammer amulet. "You will tell the gods that Sorcha's man, Brude, yet serves her well. I'll claim my mead another day!"

The taunt made, Brude roared and charged, his ax whistling in the air, ready to rain blows on Gare. Mairi felt the blood drain from her, terror washing over her in waves, chilling her like a hail of sheeting ice. The wind buffeted her and the rain drenched her, but she couldn't move, fear and dread freezing her where she stood.

When Brude raised his arm for a hacking blow to Gare's neck, she yelled, "Nae! He can have me! Stop now, please!" *I can't bear it!*

She dashed toward them, running, only to fall to her knees when Troll hurled himself at her and knocked her down. Snarling in caution, not a threat, he sat on her spread skirts, making clear he meant to guard her well.

Gare and his opponent ignored her. Their gazes were locked, the red haze of fury on their faces. Sword and ax looked bloodied, but Mairi couldn't tell for sure because of the rain and the blowing mist, which was thickening. She did hear the crash and clash of steel, the insults and grunts of the fight.

Then Brude lunged, his ax slamming into Gare's sword. The blow caused Gare to stagger, but he recovered quickly. Yelling, he scythed his sword in such a rage-filled arc that the blade cut through Brude's thick-hided bearskin and nearly severed his arm. Howling, the big man swayed and dropped to his knees, the ax slipping from his fingers. He toppled over, his blood pooling with the rain on the drenched ground.

He'd bleed out at speed, Mairi knew.

Shuddering, she reached to curl her fingers through Troll's rough fur.

"A man ne'er hurts a lady," Gare snarled, pressing the tip of his sword into the thickness of Brude's bone-hung beard. "I will tell Sorcha that you serve her no more." He nudged the long-handled ax close to the brute's hand. "Take your ax, go with your Valkyries. I'll no' be the reason any Norseman cannae enter Valhalla."

And so when Brude's fingers curled around the haft's wood, Gare nodded once.

"I will tell the gods that you fought well, whate'er I think of you," he promised, his voice strong and clear. "No Norseman should die without a weapon in his hand. And you no longer pose a threat to any woman."

Then, as Mairi watched, still too shaken to move, Gare grabbed a handful of deer grass, using it to clean the blood from his borrowed blade.

"The bastard is dead," he called over his shoulder to her. "He can harm you no more."

"Ahhh, but I can," came a dread voice behind her, just as the cold steel of a dirk's blade pressed hard against her throat. "Didn't think I'd find you, eh?"

Mairi's heart plummeted, her innards icing. She didn't need to know who'd spoken. She'd recognize the deceptively soft, eternally evil voice anywhere, anytime. There could only be one person as vile and dangerous as her nemesis.

The devil's own handmaiden.

Sorcha Bell.

~ * ~

Much later, in the smallest, darkest hours of the night, but on the far side of Kintail, light from a brace of almost gutted candles cast shadows up and down the white-washed walls of Eilean Creag Castle's most sumptuous tower bedchamber.

Quarters to the laird and his lady, the room held all the comforts a besotted husband lavishes on his much-loved wife. At the moment, Duncan MacKenzie slept deeply. His snores were light, his sleep undisturbed by the wind rattling the window shutters, the ceaseless rain drumming on his roof. He also wasn't aware of the sharp tang of brine and wet rock permeating the air.

For sure, he didn't know about the bees.

His wife, Lady Linnet, knew all about them.

She couldn't see them, but she knew why they'd wakened her with their buzzing. Somewhere beyond her capability to see them, they swarmed about the shadowy chamber, their drone increasing in volume, as did her dread.

The bees were heralds, come to warn of an impending vision.

Even after all these years, she didn't greet them gladly.

Knowing it was pretty much pointless, she went into one of the room's deep-set window embrasures and threw open the shutters, rain and wind or nae. Sometimes brisk air helped, keeping her from slipping too deeply into the images the gods chose to show her.

Now and then she suspected Duncan's powerful presence held the visions at bay. He wasn't at all fond of them. She'd noticed that whenever he was near, she was bothered less frequently.

This night he slept soundly, only the half width of the room away from her.

Which meant the vision's message was dire.

"Duncan, my love..." She glanced at him, sprawled naked across the covers as always when in their bed. Chill, wet air and moonlight spilled through the window, limning the room – and him - in a shimmering silver glow.

He truly was magnificent.

More so now than ever, which she just might tell him, and would if the bees' buzzing wasn't increasing so rapidly.

But it was.

All she could do was slump onto one of the embrasure's window seats and wait. It was already clear that the moonlight bathing the room with such silvery luminosity wasn't cast by the moon.

The silvery shaft coming through the window now speared across the chamber to merge with the light and shadows thrown on the wall by the brace of candles.

Where they met, an image was taking shape, weaving and pulsing on the wall until a silver sword appeared – hovering over the stag's head tapestry that hung above their bed!

Linnet could only stare, unable to do aught else.

But she knew who carried the sword, for its blade was broken.

Sir Gare MacTaggert.

What she didn't know was why the sword was growing.

As she watched, the blade's steel elongated, stretching longer and shining brighter until a full-length, undamaged sword hung in the air, dazzling her.

The image's brilliance hurt her eyes, but looking away from any vision risked losing the image and its message. And this one was clear.

Beautifully, wonderfully so.

Mairi had captivated the once-great knight.

She'd freed him of whatever penance he'd placed upon himself, perhaps even enjoying a bit of romance in the Glen of Winds before he returned to his duties. Obligations that she knew would see him soon wed.

She wouldn't consider more – doing so risked offending the gods that gave her such images.

The old ways must be accepted as they came. Any tampering or imposing of your own wishes bode ill, perhaps even reversing any good that might have come.

It was enough to see that Mairi had made the broken knight whole again.

Or so she thought until a red drop fell from the ceiling and trickled down the sword. Another drop followed, soon joined by more. Again and again the red rain plopped on the blade, rolling its length, catching on the hilt, and then dripping to the floor.

Linnet's eyes rounded, horror sluicing her.

The need to look away screamed inside her, but she remained frozen, unable to speak or even move. By now the entire sword was bloodied, its glistening red bringing the sharp, metallic bite of blood.

Fresh blood, newly spilled.

Linnet pressed a hand to her mouth, chilled.

She hoped she wouldn't be shown whose blood it was. But then she blinked, felt less light-headed, and the droning bees were silent, the image gone.

She was free once again.

Her husband still slumbered peacefully. Rain still drummed on the roof, the wind still howled. She could hear the slapping of waves on the rocks beneath the tower. It was a night like any other in her husband's proud isle-girt stronghold, so close to the Isle of Skye.

Peace reigned at Eilean Creag Castle.

But something was very wrong at Dunwynde.

Duncan would be furious, claiming he wasn't surprised in the least. But he'd also gather his men and ride for the glen at first light.

Linnet just hoped they wouldn't be too late.

Chapter 9

"Leave her be!" Gare roared, his blood icing at the nightmare beneath the cold, cloud-hazed moon.

Rain lashed down and winds howled, the whirling mist making it hard to see. But he did: Mairi kneeling on the sodden ground, held there by a hag who could only be Sorcha Bell, a withered old woman with spiteful eyes. She'd gripped Mairi's hair, pulling her head back, and pressing a dirk against Mairi's throat.

"Gare!" Mairi stared at him, her eyes wide. "She has a dagger!"

"No' much longer." Gare closed the space between them, cold anger tightening his chest.

Troll circled the women, growling. Rain glistened on his rough pelt and he seemed to have doubled his size. His eyes shone fiercely, his unblinking gaze on Sorcha. He'd bared his teeth, showing his large fangs so that he looked more like a wolf than a dog.

But he was well trained.

He wouldn't attack unless commanded.

"Drop the blade, Sorcha." Gare towered over them. "Now, or Troll will tear you apart. He'd savage you, and then call on his friends in the Netherworld to sharpen their teeth on you until your bones are ground to dust."

"I know you," she sneered, her gaze flicking over him. "I've seen you at cattle markets. You're the man with the broken sword."

"I carry a blade now." Gare lifted his borrowed sword, gave her his hardest look. "You just saw it in use. I've no' taste to wield it again, no' on a shriveled auld woman in a reeking deerskin cloak.

"But I will." He slid a look at Troll, nodding almost infinitesimally – a signal that had Troll on Sorcha in a beat, his great paws on her shoulders his face only a breath from hers. "You cannae win."

Sorcha sniffed. "I have the old ones' blessings. Your dog may snarl and bark, but he'll be too fearful for more. Dogs respect dark powers.

"And you, Sir Broken Sword," she jeered, "will not want to risk Mairi's neck. If your dog moves again, so does my blade."

"Indeed?" Gare drew a finger slowly down the side of his nose, a signal that brought a lightning-quick lunge from Troll. He gripped Sorcha's wrist, shaking her arm so that she dropped the dagger.

"Gare!" Mairi leapt to her feet and threw herself into his arms, holding tight.

"You are safe now, lady." He pulled her to him, tightening his arms around her. "She will be gone anon, have no fear."

"But you've vowed to not…" She pressed her head to his shoulder, not finishing.

It didn't matter.

He knew what she meant, and she was right.

He'd made an oath he couldn't break, whatever Sorcha's sins.

"I didnae say I'd kill her, only that she'll be leaving us. And she will." He brought her hand to his lips, kissing her fingers. "Sorcha!" he turned back to the hag, raised his voice above the wind. "I do no' make war on women, ever. You attack innocents. That cannae go unpunished."

"Mairi MacKenzie was born wild." Sorcha glared venom at them, shook back her whir of tightly curled red-gray hair. "There isn't an innocent bone in her body."

"You will return to Drumbell and make it your lifelong ambition to undo the wrong you've done her." Gare's temper flared. He struggled to speak levelly. "Folk will hear the truth from you and I'll know if that isn't so." He looked hard into her cold, resentful eyes. "If I must come for you, there will be no place in Scotland for you to hide.

"Go now, before the itch in my sword hand speaks faster." He stepped back, placing himself before Mairi, shielding her.

"Wait…" Mairi came round him to fix Sorcha with a look. "See that my cottage and garden are given to the young thatcher and his new wife. They are staying with his parents and need a decent home to start their lives."

Sorcha's lips thinned. "I fancied your wee hovel for a new herbarium."

"You heard the lady." Gare slid his arm around Mairi drawing her close. "See it is done, as she wishes. I will hear if you fail her."

"Humph!" Sorcha spit, and then spun around, scuttling away into the rain and mist.

She was gone in a blink.

Mairi stood shivering, Troll keeping guard beside her. She looked miserable. Dripping wet, flushed, her hair a tangled mess. Her eyes glistened in the darkness. Her drenched clothes clung to her, revealing as much as naked skin. Gare swallowed, need unfurling inside him. Never had he seen a more desirable woman, and never had he wanted one so badly.

But there was only one thing he could give her.

"Come, lady," he said, placing his hand at the small of her back and guiding her to the broch. "You need a bath to warm you and then you will sleep. We'll leave for Eilean Creag at first light."

She stopped, looking up at him. "We?"

"Aye." His mind was set. "You can stay here no longer."

They'd reached Dunwynde and she glanced at him as he pulled aside the door's curtain so she could enter the broch's smoky warmth.

"Sorcha will heed your threats." She pulled off her dripping cloak, spread it near the fire to dry. "She is a coward."

"So she is," Gare agreed, wishing she wasn't more. "Sadly, she is also a tongue-wagger. She will no' cross me, for sure. She saw what I did to her man.

"But she knows where you are." Gare fastened the door hanging, turned to face her. "One mention of the Glen of Winds and other ill-wishers could appear on your doorstep," he said, going to the back of the broch to fetch her large wooden bathing tub.

"That could be," she agreed, but something flickered in her eyes as she watched him boil water for her bath.

He wasn't sure, but he thought it was a look of hope.

Before it could grow, he braced himself to say words that would spear his heart.

A truth he knew she didn't want to hear.

"Your place is with your people." His gut clenched, everything in him warring against what he must do. "Duncan MacKenzie will keep you safe – we have discussed this. Few lairds care for their own as he does. All know it and no man, or woman, would dare cross him."

"That is so." She'd slipped into the deeper shadows, was stripping off her wet clothes behind the plaid she'd hung for privacy. "I should have stayed at Eilean Creag when I first sought his protection."

Gare nodded, busying himself with lining her wash tub with a large linen cloth, then searching her shelf for the small jar of rose-scented soap she favored. When her bath was ready, he'd bury Brude. Mairi shouldn't be confronted with such a sight when they left Dunwynde at daybreak.

The task would also spare him from the temptation of having her wet and naked before him. Her warm, welcoming self, and her lush, ripe curves only paces away, yet as unattainable as the stars.

"The Black Stag and his family will welcome me." Mairi emerged from behind the plaid hanging, a large linen drying cloth wrapped around her.

She stood near the fire, watching as he filled the tub with heated water. "He has aye said his door is always open to kin, a place aye at his table."

Gare's chest tightened with a pain he never wanted to feel again. "Then all will be well on the morrow."

Nae, it wouldn't.

Leaving Kintail without Mairi would gut him, creating an ache he'd carry forever.

He craved her, relishing the softness and warmth of her in his arms, the honeyed taste of her kiss, the silkiness of her hair. She'd also won him with her compassion, strength, and kindness. Truth was, he'd come to love her.

The sharp pain gathering in his chest at the thought of saying goodbye, proved it.

Walking away might serve the greater good of the Scottish realm, and secure the continued weal of his people at Blackrock. But it would destroy him.

All this he knew. Yet what choice did he have?

Not one that he could see.

~ * ~

A short while later, Mairi was sure the broch's dim lighting was playing tricks on her. Or the blessedly warm water of her bath had lulled her into a dream state.

How else could she explain the lovely young woman standing before her, backlit by the glow of the peat fire. She wore a man's steel-linked armor and held a plumed helmet. One hand rested on her heart, and her gaze was on Mairi, her eyes beseeching.

She shone with a light that came from within and Mairi knew who she was.

Lady Gwendolyn Berry, the ill-fated English noblewoman Gare had unknowingly struck down at the battle of Neville's Cross five years before.

Unafraid of ghosts, for what were they but the souls of once living men who'd left the earthly realm, Mairi eased up in the high-sided bathing tub. Her heart knocked wildly, whether she was accepting of bogles or nae.

Encountering one wasn't something that happened every day.

As if she understood, the spirit gave her a small, sad smile, and then glanced at the door.

Tell him... he is free.

Mairi didn't see Lady Gwendolyn's lips move, but she heard the words as surely as if the ghost had whispered them in her ear.

But then a strong gust of chill, wet wind shook the door's hanging and the room's light and shadows shifted, blurring the spirit's image. Or perhaps Lady Gwendolyn simply chose to vanish, her quest met.

Either way, Mairi knew what she had to do.

She had two parting gifts for Gare, though one was as much a present to herself.

She hoped he'd accept both.

To that end, she gripped the sides of the cloth-lined tub and pushed to her feet. Before she could reach for the drying cloth, the door's curtain was drawn back and Gare strode into the broch.

He froze, staring at her nakedness. "By thunder!" He clapped a hand to his eyes, shook his head. "I didnae mean..." The words hung between them, rough-edged and raw. "I was gone a while. I thought you'd be abed by now."

"No harm done." Mairi spoke calmly, hoped he'd think her shivering was from the night's chill and not because of his gaze on her bared flesh. A perusal that stirred her blood, rousing her. "I am not shy, not ashamed of my nakedness.

"The warm water was soothing." She took the drying cloth, began rubbing the wetness from her skin. "I stayed in the bath longer than intended."

"I should've called out before coming inside." He went to the shelf where she kept her uisge beatha, pouring two measures. He kept his back to her, clearly giving her privacy to don her night shift.

Mairi frowned, fighting the urge to go to him. She yearned to touch his broad-set shoulders, glide her fingers down her strong, hard-muscled arms. Above all, she ached to take his hand and lead him to her bed where she wanted to give him the gift she so hoped he'd accept.

One night entwined, intimately joined until the rising sun separated them.

Loving him would break her, shredding her soul.

Seeing him ride away from Kintail without having known his touch, would be a far worse fate to bear.

She needed such memories to sustain her.

So she left her night shift on its wall peg and pulled on her thin night robe instead. She tied the laces only loosely, aware that the front-opening robe did little to hide her most valuable assets.

She wanted him to see her bared curves, every enticement of her womanliness. Hoping he wouldn't turn around before she was done, she took a small flagon of rose-scented oil from a niche in the wall. Quickly, she dabbed a few drops at the base of her neck, beneath her breasts, and – she didn't care what such wantoness said about her – to the soft skin of her inner thighs and even the warm and needy place betwixt them.

Perhaps she really was wild and wicked, in need of taming as many folk at Drumbell often scolded. But she didn't see love as wrong.

Tempting Gare was her only chance.

But first…

She took a deep breath and stood straighter, pushing aside all thought of her yearnings. Now wasn't the moment to attempt seduction.

Even so, it was hard to resist as he came back to her, carrying two small cups of uisge beatha. He gave her one, his gaze steady on hers, as if he hadn't noticed the almost opened state of her bed robe – or had and didn't want to look at her.

"Drink, lady." He pressed the cup into her hand, nodding when she took a sip. "It's been a fraught night, but many of your cares can now be eased."

"So can yours, my lord," she spoke formally, the weight of what she was about to say heavy on her heart. "I believe I know why the gods led you here."

He'd just drained his uisge beatha and dragged the back of his hand across his beard. "To slay dragons? Sweet lass, I would have fought an army of the winged beasties for you. All that matters is that you are safe."

"So I am, and shall be – on the morrow, at my chief's isle-girt home." Mairi took another steadying breath. The light and shadow in the broch felt odd again, seeming to shift and swirl around them. It almost felt as if they'd entered another realm, the rest of the world falling away.

"You are safe now, too." She hoped he'd believe her. "By letting Sorcha go, you repaid the loss of Lady Gwendolyn. However unknowingly her life was taken."

"What are you saying?" He stepped closer, gripping her arm.

Mairi lifted her chin, forging on. "A balance was struck when you allowed Sorcha to walk away. Your debt, the penance you've borne, is over. I know because the lady appeared to me there." She flung out a hand, showing him where the spirit had hovered. "She wanted me to tell you that 'you are free.'"

For a long moment, he looked at the empty space she'd indicated.

"Lady, I dinnae believe in bogles," he finally said. But he was still gripping her arm and she could feel the tightness of his muscles easing, sensed that a tremendous burden was slipping from his shoulders.

"This broch is full of shifting light and shadow." He glanced round, as if to prove it. "The rain is dwindling and the clouds are breaking. You saw a moonbeam through the door opening. Lady Gwendolyn is away and buried in England."

She was here this night.

She cared enough to want you to live a good life.

Mairi didn't say what she knew.

She suspected he'd believe in time and that was enough.

Now, this night...

"I would give you one more gift to carry away with you, if-" Her bravura began to crumple. She couldn't bear it if he refused her. "I believe you've received everything you sought here, and that is good. In coming to the glen, you also brought something to me.

"Stirrings, feelings I'd never expected." Not knowing what else to do, she undid the ties of her robe and let the garment drop to the floor.

She stood naked before him, bathed only in the broch's dimness and fire glow, wholly unashamed, yet so frightened he'd shun her.

"Lady..." He clenched his hands, his gaze roaming over her, his eyes dark. "This is no good idea."

But he didn't snatch up her robe and swirl it around her as she'd expected. That gave her hope, as did the unmistakable swelling at his groin.

He clearly desired her.

And her heart sang to see his longing.

"I've been alone some time," she rushed on, the night air chilling her skin even as her cheeks burned. She swept back her hair, freeing her breasts. Molten awareness poured through her, pooling low in her belly, deep between her thighs. "You've been without the comfort of a woman for longer than I have missed a man's caress," she said, scarce hearing her voice for the thunder of her pulse. "No lover has ever kindled such heat in me."

"I know what you're offering." His expression was fierce, his entire warrior's body looking as if he'd been cast to stone. "We shouldnae do this. The price for such pleasure could be steep."

"Then you're not refusing me?" *You are worth any cost.* She stepped closer, her breasts brushing his chest. The heat of him warmed her through his plaid. "We would hurt no one..."

"Only ourselves." His eyes glinted, his words hinting at pain that was a distant blur in the future.

"I do not care – for myself." It was all she could do not to twine her arms around his neck, drawing him to her for kisses. Her fingers itched to tear the plaid from him. She wanted to run her hands over his bared skin, learning and memorizing each muscled plane, glorying in his sandalwood scent, his potent virility. "I only ask these last few hours. Then we shall be no more."

"By all the bleeding gods!" He caught her to him, his mouth crashing down over hers in a deep, devouring kiss. He thrust one hand into her hair, gripping her nape as he kissed her hungrily. It was a bold, open-mouthed claiming that stole her breath and left her clinging to him. Her heart raced, the world around her beginning to tilt and spin as she clutched his powerful, plaid-draped shoulders, returning the kiss with all the passion she possessed.

He pulled her closer, releasing her hair and using his free hand to tear off his plaid. As quickly, he tossed it aside so that not even a sliver of air stood between their eager nakedness.

"Gare?" She drew back to look at him. "My bed of furs, shall we-"

"Aye!" He scooped her into his arms and carried her to her sleeping place where he laid her on the thick pelts, then knelt beside her. He trailed his fingers across her breasts, smoothed his hand down her side, along the curve of her hip. "I have ached for this, lady, even as I swore no' to touch you."

Mairi reached up to stroke his beard. "I am feeling more a wench than a lady."

"You are my lady, and e'er shall be." His gaze swept her, so heatedly that she almost felt the breath of flames everywhere he looked. When his gaze paused at the vee of her thighs and he skimmed his fingertips across the dark curls there, she melted.

The hot pulsing in that most intimate place was nigh unbearable, her desire so great she could scarce breathe.

She wouldn't think about him calling her his lady.

She was wench enough to know men say many things in the throes of passion.

"All I want is this night." *And then a thousand more, again and again for all our days.* She trailed her fingers across his chest, admiring his sculpted muscles, the scattering of dark hair that arrowed from his chest to his belly and lower. "I would give you ease to carry with you when you go."

Moments I'll wrap in every beat of my heart, to treasure forever.

"Sweet lass." He stretched out beside her, reached to palm her breasts, plumping and caressing them. Cherishing her as if she were a great and precious prize. "You give me too much. But I am captivated and cannae resist," he said, his voice gruff as he leaned in to rain kisses across the swells of her breasts, then swirl his tongue around one peak and then the other.

Mairi's entire body warmed, tingly bliss spooling through her. Around them, light and shadow merged until nothing remained but a shimmer of silver that shielded them from the outside world as he closed his mouth over one tight nipple and drew hard, the intimacy almost pushing her over the edge.

"I didnae want this." He lifted his head to look at her as he slid his hand from her breasts to her waist, stroking lower to slip his fingers between her legs. He caressed the soft, sensitive insides of her upper thighs, then the sleek, damp place that tingled so desperately.

"I cannae naesay you." His fingers lit over her again and again, each touch bringing ribbons of pleasure.

The sensations were heady, making her rock her hips into his hand. She didn't want him to stop. She let her knees fall wider apart, opening her to his bliss-spending fingers as he sought and circled the sweetest part of her, heightening her pleasure. Yet she still craved more, was sure she'd shatter if he lifted his hand from her.

"I can take no more." She could hardly speak. "No man has ever touched me this way…"

"Nor will any ever again. You are mine, Mairi MacKenzie. I willnae let you go." His voice was low, the words again claims she knew men made when pleasuring women.

They meant nothing.

Not for a supposed wonder healer who'd been raised on an onion farm.

Her heart pounded anyway.

And she let herself hope as she looked down to watch his fingers stroke her.

"You are beautiful, more dear than a King's ransom." He used one finger to rub the tiny seat of her greatest pleasure. "I could touch and kiss you all night, ravishing every inch of you.

"Especially this part." He splayed his hand over her, cupping the whole of her.

Mairi shivered, her blood racing. "You may have anything you desire. I am yours, this night." *Don't leave me on the morrow.*

I can't watch you go.

"I would have you, aye," he vowed, his gaze on the place he was still gripping so firmly. "So sure as a man cannae hold back the tide."

Then he was nudging her knees even wider and settled himself between her thighs, leaning down until his breath warmed her skin. He eased her legs over his shoulders, his gaze lifting to hers as he lowered his head and flicked his tongue over the delicate flesh where his fingers had plied such mastery. He circled and probed, then simply began licking her. Long, slow drags of his tongue across the whole of her, again and again, so that the sweetest, most intense pleasure speared through her. Beautiful sensations she'd never known and that she couldn't bear to relinquish.

"Gare..." She lifted her hips, threaded her fingers in his hair as she rubbed against him, already feeling the crest of her release. "I can take no more."

"You can, and shall." He opened his mouth over her, drawing deeply, causing her hips to arch at the intimacy. "I willnae stop until we are both replete. You are nowhere near sated enough. We have hours before the sun rises."

Mairi's heart broke, the reminder of the morrow piercing her soul.

"Then take me now and let us love well." She smoothed her hands over his head, cradled his face. "I would have you at least three times before the morn's light."

"No' near enough." He rolled on top her and she felt the hard, thick length of him against her inner thigh, nudging her needy flesh, seeking entry.

He braced himself above her and lowered his head, slanting his mouth over hers and kissing her deeply as he eased inside her. Slowly at first, but then she wrapped her legs around him, drawing him deeper. She gripped his shoulders, urging him into a harder, faster rhythm that took her breath and made her heart pound.

She clung to him, the pleasure so intense, more exquisite than she would've believed. And all around them the strange and beautiful silvery light danced and shone, intensifying when he reached down between them to rub and circle her most sensitive spot until the sensations spiraled and broke. Her body quivered and then stilled, waves of completion washing over her.

From somewhere, she thought she heard him call her name. She wasn't sure, for the wind was rising again, its howl louder than ever.

But then he slowed and heaved a great, shuddering breath as he pulled out of her. He rolled onto his back, drawing her close against his side. She rested her head on his shoulder, slid one leg over his hip.

"Sweet lass." He smoothed back her hair, kissed her brow. "I would ne'er hurt you."

You already have – by leaving. "You have only brought me joy." Mairi allowed herself the half-truth, not wanting to speak of the sorrow to come. "I did not know such pleasure existed. Not as with you."

"You deserve so much more." He pushed up on an elbow just as the door curtain moved and Troll entered the broch.

"He left us alone, didn't he?" Mairi watched the dog walk without a limp to his food bowl, polishing his evening meal and then drinking deeply from his water.

Troll knew there was no more reason to feign ailments or achy bones.

He'd accepted defeat, sensed they were leaving.

"He's a smart lad." Gare took her hand, lacing their fingers. "He'll be at the door when the first hint of gray lightens the sky."

"And you?" She held her breath.

"I shall be there before him." He gave her the answer she'd dreaded.

Mairi turned her face to the side and drew a long, tight breath. She needed to steel herself against the memories they'd just made.

How could she have believed they'd be enough?

Chapter 10

Early the next morning, high the most barren region of Kintail's greatest peaks, Gare sent a prayer to the gods. He thanked them that he'd wakened with Mairi beside him. Whatever the day brought, he'd have the memory of her wrapped in arms, her warmth pressed to him, her silky black hair streaming across his chest.

She'd even rested her hand atop his heart, as if she knew it beat only for her.

Remembering, his chest tightened, so he pushed the images from his mind. What he needed to do was keep putting one foot before the other as they trudged across yet another bleak, wind-bitten ridge.

They'd set off early and the Glen of Winds was now far behind them as they made their way across the stony, mist-drenched heights of Kintail toward Duncan MacKenzie's stronghold, the isle-girt castle, Eilean Creag.

Gare frowned, dreading what would happen there.

But Mairi's safety and happiness were at stake. And he didn't want her damned.

Above all, he didn't want to lose her.

The need to keep her at his side was powerful, a driving force that could destroy them both.

He glanced over his shoulder at the way they'd come. His gaze couldn't pierce the wall of mist swirling everywhere, but he felt Dunwynde behind him, its peat-hazed warmth and solace. How he wished they could've stayed there, hidden away in Mairi's bed of furs. The haven where he'd learned how much he loved her, how fiercely he wanted to keep her.

"Are you sure this is the way?" She touched his arm, looking at him with worry in her great blue eyes. "I'm not concerned for myself," she said, glancing at Troll. "But Troll will need a rest before we go much farther."

"Then we'll pause here for a bit." Gare didn't like how she'd set a hand on her hip, drawing in long, deep breaths of the chill autumn air.

She looked exhausted and that only heaped more worry and guilt on his shoulders.

Especially as he knew she hadn't slept, a lacking that was his fault entirely – much as he couldn't deny she'd been equally ravenous.

Mairi MacKenzie was insatiable.

She was incomparable. Wild, uninhibited, and more passionate than any woman he'd ever known.

Her heart...

He doubted the world's great seas could contain her goodness, the deep compassion that beat inside her.

"It isnae much farther," he said, pulling her to him, rubbing her back, hoping to soothe her weariness as best he could. "My regrets that we left so early, and in such miserable conditions." He dropped a kiss on her brow, glanced again at the mist that had thickened since they'd reached the higher ground. "At least the rains have ceased."

"How can you know we're close?" She rested her head on his shoulder. "We can see nothing."

"I know as any Highlander does." He cupped her chin, leaning down to give her a soft, light kiss.

And he did know.

To the bone, he was aware of the great stony peaks soaring around them. He knew they were there because his love for the land let him feel their mighty presence. They just couldn't be seen. Thick, impenetrable mist cloaked them completely, parting only now and then to allow glimpses of rock-clogged corries, steep gorges, patches of brown-and-red bracken, dead heather, and rushing burns.

This was the heart of the Highlands, Kintail the lifeblood of the region.

Then, before they could see more, the day turned dark and bleak again, the world vanishing beneath the rolling blanket of dense, gray fog.

Mairi rubbed her arms, drew her cloak tighter against the icy air. "I do not want to spend the night up here. Troll will catch a chill."

"Troll will sleep before your laird's hearth fire this night, his belly full, and his snores annoying everyone. Dinnae fash yourself, lassie."

"Well, I do."

"You needn't. I can smell the sea wind." He turned her in his arms, set his hands on her shoulders. "I spent too many years sailing to the gods knows where on the tourney circuit. Once you've steeped your lungs in salt air, you have a nose for it, always."

"Troll isn't so certain." Mairi glanced at the dog. He'd dropped onto his haunches, looking miserable.

"He wasn't with me in those days." He stepped away from her to pull a small pouch from beneath his cloak, retrieving a twist of dried meat that he gave to Troll, clearly a bribe.

"He will be fine, as will you. Soon." He tucked the treat pouch back inside his cloak. "Eilean Creag Castle is less than an hour's walk, I promise."

She nudged a clump of autumn-browned heather with her toe, clearly not convinced.

"You dinnae believe me." Gare touched her cheek. "Look between thon drifts of mist, and then down the slope to the west. You will see the glimmer of torchlight and hearth fires."

He turned her in the right direction. "The firelight is also shining on the water, turning it orange. Thon is your laird's stronghold, with Loch Duich surrounding its walls."

"Aye, I see the castle now. It is Eilean Creag." She whipped around, strong emotion in her face. "Will you be leaving this day? For Burnett Tower in Inverness?"

Before he could answer, Troll leapt to his feet, barking.

At once, the air filled with the shouts of men. Someone blew a horn, once and then twice more. The sound echoed off the high crags as the misty wood came alive, the noise of approaching horsemen all around them. Iron-shod hooves rang on stone, joined by the crunch of gravel and the creak of saddle leather, the clink of mail and armor.

"Mercy!" Mairi gripped Gare's arm. "Can Sorcha be returning so soon? With an army?"

"No' if she doesnae want her gizzards pickled." Gare pulled her behind him and drew Brude's borrowed sword. Ever a champion, Troll positioned himself beside Mairi, ready to guard her. "Whoe'er comes is no' from that hag. Even so, you take this ax and use it if you can." He pulled Brude's war ax from the strap across his shoulder, and thrust it into her hands. "The sight of it should deter a man – leastways long enough for Troll to tear out his throat, should anyone come at you."

"If you are gone." She spoke so softly he scarce heard her.

"Should that happen, aye." He wouldn't lie. "I'm hoping it willnae come to that. Like as no' they are headed elsewhere and havenae seen us."

Mairi didn't look so sure.

In truth, he wasn't either.

He drew her into his arms, holding her close. "Perhaps it is your Sir Marmaduke and his men?"

"Nae, it wouldn't be." She shook her head. "This is the fastest, most direct way into the Glen of Winds, but also the roughest. Traveling these passes would be too hard on my chief's horses. He wouldn't want the beasts so stressed or endangered.

"Sir Marmaduke and his men use a safer, more circuitous route." She looked up, turning her blue gaze on him. "They'd never come this way."

"Then Troll and I will keep you safe." His voice roughened. "You know that now." He rested his chin atop her head, tightened his arms around her. "You'll spend this night in a fine chamber in your liege's castle, a room with sumptuous accoutrements and all comfort, as befits you.

"That I promise." He kissed her rose-scented hair, slid his knuckles down her cheek.

She shivered and pressed her face against his plaid, but she didn't speak.

There wasn't time.

The sounds were closer. Already, flashes of silver shone through the trees. Steel blades and mail, sure signs of a war party – then they were there, a group of horsemen emerging from the trees. Big, bearded men in gleaming hauberks and draped in plaid, they were hung with weapons and rode under a stag's head banner.

MacKenzies.

And from their hard, grim-set faces, the reason for their journey wasn't good.

Indeed, they looked murderous.

~ * ~

"My chief!" Mairi glanced at Gare, saw an indefinable emotion flash across his face. "He's the big, dark-haired man in front, the one with two swords at his waist. Next to him is his captain of the guards, Sir Marmaduke Strongbow. He's Duncan's good-brother by marriage and a Sassenach. You can't miss him – his face is scarred."

"Then they'll have reason to travel so heavily armed." Gare rammed his borrowed blade into the ground, waiting. "I dinnae think they expected to meet us here."

"Maybe they heard of Sorcha's attack?" Mairi could think of nothing else.

Still in his prime, Duncan's handsome face was fierce, his gaze piercing. He'd donned his famed black mail and looked more fearsome than she'd ever seen him, while the heavy gold torque at his neck and his many gold-and-silver arm rings gave him the appearance of a Celtic lord of warriors.

His good-brother, the more mild-mannered Sir Marmaduke, also wore a grim expression.

Whatever their purpose, they weren't on their way to bring victuals or peat to Dunwynde.

Both men swung down from their saddles and strode forward. Their companions stayed mounted, their faces also unreadable.

Ill ease spread inside Mairi. She pressed a hand to her breast, her heart knocking against her ribs.

She slid a glance at Gare, lowering her voice. "Something is wrong."

"So it seems." He reached for her hand, squeezing. "I have heard MacKenzie is a man of reason – if you speak plainly with him. I shall do so."

Mairi bit her lip, struggling to control her emotions.

She knew what that truth would be.

And hearing him voice his plans would break her.

"Laird MacKenzie! Strongbow! I greet you!" Gare called as they drew up before them. "I am Sir Gare MacTaggert of Blackrock Castle. I came to your lands in peace and leave them now as a friend," he went on, proving her right.

He flashed a glance at her and she hoped he didn't see the wetness burning her eyes. "Your kinswoman, Mairi, is in need of safekeeping. We were on our way to Eilean Creag Castle, where my horse, Rune is stabled. I would ask a night's lodging, and-"

"You carry a sword, Blackrock." Duncan didn't let him finish, his gaze snapping to the blade Gare had thrust into the ground. "All men know your sword is broken – or is it now bloodied?"

"The sword you see was reddened, aye. Yestere'en." Gare didn't flinch, meeting the older man's gaze easily. "My rent blade rests beneath a cairn in the Glen of Winds for I've no longer any use for it. This brand" – he indicated Brude's weapon – "is borrowed until I return to my home and can have a new sword made.

"Borrowed or nae, it served me well last night," he added, then reached again for Mairi's hand, lacing their fingers as he told her chief of Sorcha's attack and how he slew their assailant. He left out no detail except what happened later, in the shadowy confines of Mairi's broch, on her fine bed of furs.

"Sir…" Mairi wished Duncan's scowl would ease. He looked so fierce when he frowned. "If Gare hadn't been with me in the glen, I would be dead now. He was taking me to you, trusting it is best for me to leave Dunwynde and stay at Eilean Creag, under your protection."

"Is that what you want?" Sir Marmaduke stepped closer and looked down at her, his gaze probing. "To remain at Eilean Creag?"

"It is surely best." She glanced aside, not wanting him to see into her heart.

Stinging heat pricked her eyes and a hot, thick lump was rising in her throat. Worse, she felt so cold inside, empty and hollowed. She feared she'd never be whole again.

She loved Duncan and his family. But she wanted her own. Unfortunately, she desired a life with the one man she couldn't have. And arriving at the Black Stag's lair only meant impending doom.

Sanctuary for her or nae, Eilean Creag Castle represented the hour of reckoning. The agonizing moment when she'd have to watch Gare ride off into the mist.

It was not for the best.

But her pride wouldn't let her say so.

She did see Duncan and Sir Marmaduke exchange a glance. It was the kind she'd seen before, usually when Lady Linnet had been after the two of them about something.

Just now, she suspected that something was her.

"And you, laddie?" Duncan strode up to Gare, clapped a hand on his shoulder. "Are you for agreeing that Mairi would be best served in my care?"

Gare didn't hesitate. "She would be safe with you, I know."

"But that's no' what you're wanting, is it?" Duncan's gaze flicked to where Gare clutched Mairi's hand. When he looked back at Gare, his scowl was gone, replaced by an almost smile that tugged at the corner of his mouth.

"My lady wife, Linnet, has the sight, see you?" He stepped closer still, placed his other hand on Mairi's shoulder, forming a connection to them both. "My lady is why we were riding so hard for the glen, armed for war. She had one of her spells last night, claimed she saw your broken sword run whole and then turn red with blood.

"She had other tales as well, though I'll no' be sharing those!" He threw a glance at Sir Marmaduke, who had the good grace to look embarrassed.

"So-o-o!" He stepped back, hooking his thumbs in his sword belt. "I'll ask again, laddie. Are you really for leaving the lass at my castle?"

"Nae, I'm taking her with me – whether it pleases you or no'." Gare drew her close, wrapping an arm around her. "I haven't asked her yet if she'll have me, though I'm thinking she will. There are problems I intended to speak with you about before I asked you for her hand."

"Oh, Gare!" Mairi searched his face for any hint that she'd misheard him. She saw none, only love and determination. "You know how happy this makes me. I love you, I do!"

She lifted on her toes, threw her arms around his neck, kissing his cheek. "But Lady Beatrice..." She knew it would be awful, especially if they called at Burnett Tower together. "Her family will be outraged, insulted-"

"Nae, they willnae." He leaned down, kissed her brow. "I ne'er paid a formal call to the Burnett. His daughter was only the most suitable of the young gentlewomen suggested to me as a bride. I didn't want to claim any woman until I'd seen you, knew that I could rid myself of my penance and make a good husband."

"So she never knew?" Mairi's heart thundered, her eyes filling, hot tears making it hard to see. "You weren't betrothed to her?"

"Nae." Gare smiled, shaking his head. "I meant to call at Burnett Tower on my journey home. Now there is no need."

"Then what is the problem?" Sir Marmaduke still looked concerned.

Duncan glared at him. "Must you aye spoil happy endings?"

Unperturbed, the scar-faced Sassenach turned again to Gare. "Tell us what else troubles you, lad. Here in Kintail, there is little thon blowhard cannot fix."

"Aye, right..." Gare stepped away from the little group, rubbing his neck as he started pacing. "That is the crux of it, see you?" He glanced at the two older men, not looking at Mairi. "The matter is delicate and I'd no' hurt Mairi for all the world's gold."

"So?" Duncan and Sir Marmaduke spoke in unison, both men folding their arms.

"'Twas an order from the King's Lieutenant, Robert Stewart, commanding me to wed," Gare explained, going on to tell them the same tale he'd already shared with Mairi. How the crown wished Scotland's oft-times unruly northeastern corner better secured through strong alliances. For Gare, that meant marriage to a daughter of good house, a well-seen family of noble blood and one that commanded respect.

Mairi struggled to keep standing where she was. She felt a powerful urge to flee, to run all the way back to Dunwynde. It was even harder not to thrust her fingers in her ears. Gare might love her, and she was sure he did. But she was still the daughter of a nameless father, a simple village lass raised by her aunt and uncle, the onion farmers.

Nothing could change that.

So why was her chief smiling, looking almost amused?

"That is no problem, lad," Duncan boomed then, strolling over to Gare and putting his arm around Gare's shoulders. "See you, I have ne'er cared much for Lowland worthies, those who strut about Stirling and Edinburgh, garbed like peacocks and shrieking as loudly. I've no mind to obey them. No' when it doesnae suit me." He paused, threw a look at his men over by the trees, the lot of them still mounted.

"But I will rally to their cause if doing so helps strengthen a region my beloved Lady Mairi might soon call her home."

"Sir?" Mairi blinked. She glanced at Gare, saw he looked equally puzzled. "Gare knows I am not a lady. I didn't lie to him."

Now Sir Marmaduke was also smiling. "Sweet Mairi," he said, his dear voice gentle, "you need to listen with your heart and not your ears."

Mairi pushed back her hair, still confused. "I don't understand. Sorry, I-"

"Your chief called you Lady Mairi." Gare was suddenly beside her, his own eyes suspiciously moist. He leaned in, lowering his voice. "I believe it has something to do with his Sassenach captain saying he makes his own rules and does as he pleases here in his beloved Kintail."

And then she understood.

"Oh, dear…" She blinked furiously, unable to stop the tears spilling down her cheeks.

"Here, lass." Sir Marmaduke was beside her then, pressing a small, linen cloth into her hand. "Dry your tears, for you've no need to cry."

"For sure, she doesnae!" Duncan took her hand, holding it between both of his. "Nae more, and ne'er again, something's telling me."

He looked down at her and she almost laughed because his eyes were glistening, too. Then he turned again to his guards and lifted his voice, "Ho, men! We're away for home. We'll have guests in the hall this e'en. My lady niece and her husband-to-be will join us for a fine feasting! We'll have warmed mead and venison, and my best musicians for dancing."

A great cheer rose from the men and they rode forward, circling the little group as they whooped and brandished their swords, some blowing horns.

All beamed and shouted hoorahs, their excitement catching.

Not a one questioned that the onion farmer's niece was now the much-loved and privileged niece to one of the greatest Highland chieftains Scotland had ever seen.

Indeed, no one would dare raise a question or objection.

Not if they valued their neck.

And so it came to be that, on a cold and mist-drenched morning, the Glen of Winds banshee ceased to exist.

Even so, it was a bit hard saying farewell to her. Without the banshee, or the wonder healer, Gare would never have journeyed to Dunwynde.

"Then we would have met elsewhere, my love." He stepped up behind her, sliding his arms around her and pulling her back against him.

They needed to wait while Duncan's men argued who would have the honor of giving up their mount so the laird's lady niece could return to Eilean Creag in style.

"I can't speak – I am so overcome," she managed, leaning into him, hoping her knees wouldn't buckle. "What if you'd never sought the banshee, the caster of miracles?"

"I'd have found you if I'd had to search all broad Scotland and beyond." He dropped a kiss on her nape, his warm breath tickling her ear. "I knew you were out there, waiting for me."

His words made her heart flutter. "For such a great warrior, you are a romantic, Sir Gare."

"Only for you, Lady Mairi." He kissed her shoulder then, nipped the soft skin beneath her ear. "I would fight any dragon, challenge the devil, if it pleased you."

"You please me," she vowed, turning to face him.

"I have only one regret." He lifted her chin and kissed her. "That I waited so long to find you." He would've said more, but Troll was pushing between them, pressing into their legs, seeking attention.

The reason was apparent – they had an audience.

Duncan, Sir Marmaduke, and the guardsmen, stood in a circle around them. All of the men had tellingly bright eyes and red noses. They no longer looked fierce, but rather comical. And they were still smiling. One patiently held the horse chosen for Mairi.

It was time to go.

Even so, she grabbed Gare's sleeve when he started forward. "I have a regret, too." She spoke low, not wanting anyone else to hear. "I should have liked to have kept my bed of furs."

"You willnae need it, sweetness." He took her hand, leading her to the horse. "I will warm you every night." He brought her hand to his lips, kissing her fingertips. "I'll make sure you're so well heated you willnae want any covers."

"I know." She did.

"But?" The concern in Gare's eyes made her heart turn over. "Something still troubles you."

"Oh, nae." She placed a finger to his lips, silencing him before he could say suchlike again. "I have never been happier. It's just that I would've enjoyed having the pelts as a keepsake. Because it was there, on my bed of furs, that we first-"

"I will send someone to fetch them." He touched her face, smoothed the dampness from her cheek. "It will be my first task upon reaching Blackrock. Would that please you?"

"Oh, aye!" Mairi smiled. Her joy was now complete.

More than she'd ever dreamed.

Except...

She tugged on his hand again, lifting on her toes to speak in his ear. "There's one more thing," she said, only half teasing. "I wish my chief wasn't throwing a feast for us tonight. Free flowing mead and pipers and fiddlers could make for a long evening."

Gare arched a brow, a wicked gleam in his eyes. "Shall we slip away early?"

Mairi nodded, already tingling. "I would like that very much."

Gare grinned. "So would I, lass, so would I."

And so they did, stealing away as soon as they could that night, not caring if anyone noticed. Only Troll knew and he wasn't telling.

About the Author

"Welfonder brings legends and love to life." -
Fresh Fiction

USA Today bestselling author Sue-Ellen Welfonder won Romantic Times Best Historical Romance Award for her debut title, Devil in a Kilt. Since then, many of her books have been RT Award nominees, and most have received RT Top Picks and K.I.S.S. Hero Awards. Her favorite reader compliment is that her stories transport them to medieval Scotland, the setting of most of her books. She is known for her strong heroines, Alpha heroes, and weaving Highland magic and humor into her tales.

Sue-Ellen also writes as Allie Mackay, penning contemporary paranormals, mostly set in the Scottish Highlands.

Visit Sue-Ellen online:
facebook.com/SueEllenWelfonderAuthor
website: www.welfonder.com
Twitter: @se_welfonder

About the Scrolls of Cridhe Highland Winds – Volume 1

If you enjoyed *The Taming of Mairi Mackenzi*, you might enjoy the other novellas in Highland Winds – The Scrolls of Cridhe Volume 1

In addition to *The Taming of Mairi Mackenzie* the collection contains the following:

Highland Revenge – by Ceci Giltenan

Hatred lives and breathes between medieval clans who often don't remember why feuds began in the shadowed past.

But Eoin MacKay remembers.

He will never forget how he was treated by Bhaltair MacNicol—the acting head of Clan MacNicol. He was lucky to escape alive, and vows to have revenge.

Years later, as laird of Clan MacKay, he gets his chance when he captures Lady Fiona MacNicol. His desire for revenge is strong but he is beguiled by his captive. Can he forget his stubborn hatred long enough to listen to the secret she has kept for so long? And once he knows the truth, can he show her she is not alone and forsaken? In the end, is he strong enough to fight the combined hostilities and age-old grudges that demand he give her up?

Stealing Moirra's Heart – by Suzan Tisdale

Thrice widowed Moirra Dundotter needs a husband. With a reputation for losing husbands, the men of Glenkirby are not exactly lining up. Just as she is ready to give up, Moirra happens upon a very handsome man--locked in the village pillory.

Desperate to be free of the pillory, the stranger reluctantly agrees to handfast with Moirra, but refuses to tell her his real name -- or much else about his past. He'll stay only long enough to help her harvest crops in the fall. Two months. And not one day longer.

Fate oft has far different plans.

Spirit Stones – by Kate Robbins

Connected to the spirit world, Sheona engages with souls long departed. When in the midst of a vicious battle, she is captured by her bitter enemy. Armed with only her gift, can she escape his clutches?

Malcolm MacDonald seeks change. Exhausted from the ancient feud with the MacLeods, Malcolm sees no future for any of them until his enemy's intoxicating daughter stirs a desire for peace that drives him to risk everything—except her.

Together, they can change destiny—if they dare.

A Tear for Memory – by Kathryn Lynn Davis

Celia Rose lives happily in Fairies' Haven, where the lies that protect her from the past keep the fairies away. She finds her only magic when she paints. Then a stranger comes on a mysterious errand, showing her new colors and new passions. But he also brings danger, and is not what he seems. Can Celia trust him enough to learn the dark secret that could both destroy her innocence and forge in her a woman's heart?

A Jewel in the Vaults – by **Lily Baldwin**

In 1802, Edinburgh's poverty-ridden Old Town is rife with danger. To safeguard herself, Robbie conceals her femininity--to all the world she is a lad, but beneath the ruse is a woman aching to break free.

In pursuit of his prodigal brother, Conall MacKay solicits the aid of a young street lad named Robbie. But Conall soon realizes that there is more to both Robbie and Edinburgh's Old Town than meets the eye.

In a world where wickedness governs and darkness reigns, a savage struggle for dignity, survival, and love begins.

Lord Grayson's Bride – by **Tarah Scott**

Nicholas Spencer, Earl of Grayson, won't make the same mistake twice and let Josephine Knightly go. She loves him. He felt it in their one kiss before he left, and in the single kiss she allowed since his return. But she's doing everything in her power to sabotage the marriage even before it's begun. Nicholas doesn't care. If Hell is where he must live to have her, then she must stand by his side in the fire.

More from Sue-Ellen Welfonder

The Ravenscraig Legacy Series

Written as Allie Mackay

Time Travel/Paranormal Scottish Romance Novels

Highlander in Her Bed (Book 1)

Tour guide Mara MacDougall stops at a London antique shop-and spots perhaps the handsomest bed ever. Then she bumps into the handsomest man ever. Soon Mara can't forget the irresistible-if haughty-Highlander. Not even when she learns that she's inherited a Scottish castle.

Spectral Sir Alexander Douglas has hated the Clan MacDougall since he was a medieval knight and they tricked him into a curse-the curse of forever haunting the bed (the very one that Mara now owns) that was once intended for his would-be bride. But Mara makes him feel what no other MacDougall has-a passion that he never knew he'd missed.

Highlander in Her Dreams (Book 2)

They met through Highland Magic, can true love keep them together?

After stepping through a magical gateway, Kira Bedwell finds herself in fourteenth century Scotland, face-to-face with Aidan MacDonald, the irresistible Highlander who has visited her in dreams. Now that their romance transcends dreams to reality, they find themselves under attack by Aidan's enemies. And it will take all of their courage and will for their love to survive beyond time itself...

Aidan is a Romantic Times K.I.S.S of the Month Hero!

Tall, Dark and Kilted (Book 3)

A good man is hard to find.

Cilla Swanner has been jilted by her lover, and she is struggling with a jewelry business that's far from sparkling. She needs a getaway someplace quiet and remote. Someplace like Dunroamin Castle in Scotland, where her aunt and uncle run a retirement home in the majestic Highlands. But what she finds there may be more than she can handle.

Or is it the other way around?

Centuries ago, the roguish Scots knight known as Hardwick was renowned for his swordmanship, both on and off the battlefield. But a traveling bard cursed him to wander the world forever, pleasing a different woman each night with no hope of fulfillment or true love. Then Hardwick meets Cilla, who may be his only chance for salvation.

Some Like it Kilted (Book 4)

A ghost's home is his castle – and she's about the storm the gates.

A woman's heart needs a loving home.

Mindy Menlove lives in a castle that was transported stone by stone from Scotland to Pennsylvania. When her fiancé dies in scandal and Mindy decides to sell the gloomy estate, her plans soon unravel. She's bound for the Hebrides, a place she'd hoped to avoid. And rather than escaping the past, she'd confronted by the castle's original builder, who happens to be maddeningly irresistible and seven hundred years young.

Bran of Barra was a legendary Highland chieftain. Since his demise he has enjoyed his ghostly pleasures – until a feisty female from across the Atlantic claims that she's demolished and now intends to restore his ancestral home. It's a task she hasn't accepted willingly, and if the roguish Bran doesn't change Mindy's mind about his bonnie homeland – and him – neither of them will ever find any peace. But unexpected passion can be the most powerful...

Novellas by Sue-Ellen Wellfonder

These short novellas were originally published in Mammoth anthologies of short stories (Falling in Time: Mammoth Book of Time Travel Romance / 2009 / Running Press; The Seventh Sister: the Mammoth Book of Irish Romance / 2010 / Running Press).

Falling in Time

Aspiring writer Lindy Lovejoy knows all about happy endings. But when she travels to Scotland to research Celtic myth and lore, she never expected a chance to live her own storybook romance, until a stop at mystical Smoo Cave whisks her back in time and into the arms of Rogan MacGraith, a Highland hero who'd burn up the pages of the steamiest Scottish romance novel.

The Seventh Sister

In The Seventh Sister, down-on-her-luck American artist Maggie Gleason returns to Ireland, hoping to put old hurts behind her. Instead, revisiting the fishing village that enchanted her twelve years before only reopens wounds – until the unexpected appearance of roguish pub owner Conall Flanagan proves that the Ancient Isle is a magical place where anything can happen and true love always stands the test of time.